# THE LADY'S AMBITION

## ANNE R BAILEY

Inkblot Press

*For my Family*

*Alas! That ever prison strong*
*Should such two lovers separate,*
*Yet though our bodies suffereth wrong,*
*Our hearts should be of one estate.*

*I will not swerve, I you assure,*
*For gold nor yet for worldly fear,*
*But like as iron I will endure,*
*Such faithful love to you I bear.*

*Thus fare thee well, to me most dear*
*Of all the world, both most and least,*
*I pray you be of right good cheer*
*And think on me who loves you best.*

*And I will promise you again,*
*To think of you I will not let,*
*For nothing could release my pain*
*But to think on you my lover sweet.*

-Lady Margaret Douglas

# PART ONE

# CHAPTER 1

## 1545

MARGARET DROWNED out their prayers and calming words of encouragement with her screams. She hated them. She hated this. She hated him.

She would go on screaming until she felt she had no breath left. She was utterly spent.

"Don't fight it. Push."

The words of the midwife at her side finally penetrated her mind. She felt another contraction coming.

"Push," the woman urged her.

She wanted to say she didn't have the strength, but she couldn't bring herself to speak. Some inner untapped strength forced her to do as the woman commanded.

"That's it, milady!"

There were more screams and finally silence before another piteously quiet cry joined her own.

"A boy! A live boy, your ladyship!" The women in the room shouted gleefully. Though Margaret was elated, she was fighting through a fog of pain to try to speak.

Already servants were passing around mugs of hot ale.

The midwife who had held up her son to her was busy cleaning him and wrapping him in swaddling bands. A wet nurse was standing by ready to feed him. Margaret saw all this frantic activity through tear stained eyes. Her vision so blurred that by some tragic accident she couldn't quite make out her son in the darkened room. He appeared to her almost as though he was a ghostly apparition. A moment later he was gone from her field of vision.

"Where did he go?" she asked as a woman pressed a cup to her lips.

"To see his father. Bless his soul, your husband has been pacing the corridors outside your rooms while you worked to bring his son into the world. See how God rewards you?"

"He is healthy?"

"He is."

The words comforted her. He had arrived early into this world, and she was concerned he would not survive. She desperately wished to slip into the oblivion of sleep, but something told her to stay awake.

"You must bring him to me."

"Of course, my lady." The woman gave her a knowing smile. "But he must feed and you shall have to rest. You have suffered greatly to bring him into the world. Don't you want to rest now? We shall wash you and put you in a bed with fresh linen."

Margaret shook her head.

"Bring him to me."

The woman looked as though she would argue but then shrugged. "As you wish."

It was not long before her son was placed in her arms. His face was red as he went on crying. It made her laugh. He was crying as much as she had cried to bring him into this world.

"Hush, my little angel." She kissed his little head. "Hush now my little prince." She whispered this so low that no one could hear.

———

It took her weeks to recover.

Her husband, Matthew Stuart, Earl of Lennox, broke convention and visited her confinement chambers after she had slept and recovered her wits. He held her close, stroking her head whispering how thankful he was to have such a brave strong wife. They were blessed.

He was not the only one to repeat the same sentiment.

She was told repeatedly it was a miracle she had even been able to give birth to a healthy child.

At the age of thirty she was old to be having her first. She had spent many sleepless nights dwelling on the fate suffered by women who died in childbirth though they had been younger and stronger than herself.

She had nothing to do now but wait and dwell on her thoughts and make plans for the future.

The uncertainty and fear of childbirth was behind her now.

She had faced another great challenge and, like always, managed to weasel her way out of trouble.

She often wondered if she should change her coat of arms to display a weasel and not a prancing lion. She had been in and out of the prison all her life. She had joked with her husband once when she recounted her many imprisonments that she should have a wing of the Tower named after her.

"My sweet, don't say such things. Your luck is bound to run out," he said.

But Margaret, brazen as ever, tutted. "It shall never run dry."

She kissed him as though to prove her point. "But I do feel frightened for you. Those closest to me have suffered on my behalf, and I worry you shall as well."

"Nonsense."

She let him scoff but she had not been joking. Indeed, she worried about her husband, and now she had another creature to worry about as well; her sweet little son might be doomed by his relation to her.

She remembered sweet Tom who perished for love of her.

Those days had long since passed, but she would never forget the longing and suffering she had felt.

She still had the poems he wrote to her tucked away in a secret box.

She had found happiness in the arms of her husband

many years later, but she could never forget her first love — her first disaster.

It would be a long time before she could be churched and leave the confinement rooms at Stepheny Palace.

Margaret found herself growing stronger with each passing day. But as her strength returned, her boredom did as well. She wasn't meant to be cooped up in a room. One would think with her previous escapades she would have learned to bear imprisonment with a patient heart but it was not so.

Her husband left for Scotland shortly after she had been churched and their baby christened Henry, Lord Darnley — the name given to all the Lennox heirs. She was a proud mother, but still she languished for days in a sour state after her husband departed.

Her uncle was exacting the most he could out of his treaty with poor Mathieu. Margaret felt it was cruel to keep them separated like this. She had spoken to her husband often about asking the King for a reprieve, but he kissed her brow and told her this was his duty.

Though he showed her a brave face, Margaret knew he was fighting his own skepticism. He was not given enough men, and the King's commands to exact terrible cruelty upon the Scots were making him hated by his own countrymen.

Her little son was thriving in the nursery. The Lady Mary had sent him a beautiful gown lined with gold lace inlaid with small rubies. A gown fit for royalty.

Marveling at her son did not keep her occupied for long. Nor did the gifts she received from friends and family bring her as much satisfaction as she would've liked either.

They were at a standstill once more.

Henry was still too young to be moved to their home at Temple Newsham, and she was too lonely in Stepheny.

Finally, she traveled to London to join the court at the Queen's invitation. She was not in the mood to masque nor dance without her husband present, but she enjoyed the rich food and the company of other ladies.

Queen Katherine who had seemed so cautious in her first days as Queen now seemed to bask in the attention of the nobles around her. She had ruled successfully as regent while the King was fighting the French and had won much praise and acclaim among her peers.

Margaret wondered if she knew she should be on her guard now more than ever. The King did not like success, and when he felt someone had risen too high, he liked to bring them down.

Many had fallen victim to his anger.

Herself included.

It irked her how her uncle could greet her so nonchalantly when he had imprisoned her on many occasions for several years at a time. The fact she had almost died because of his cruelty did not seem to phase him.

"You are looking well. Have you finally left your writing desk and gone outdoors?" he said.

She was in high spirits and felt brave enough not to curb her tongue.

"I would have gone outdoors more often in the past if I had not been kept under lock and key."

There was a moment of silence as all eyes turned to the King to see how he would react to her snide comment. But she had said it with such a mischievous tone that he did not take it as a criticism or complaint. Thus, the tension was broken with the sound of his laugh.

When she wasn't out riding with the court or attending the Queen in her chambers, she met with her secretary to outline a plan for the rebuilding she had envisioned for Temple Newsham.

The kitchens would have to be torn out and rebuilt. She wished for new rooms decorated in the modern style.

"There is brick work to be repaired on the walls before you continue with any other plans." Thomas Bishop, her secretary, interrupted her long list of improvements.

"Then it shall be repaired." Margaret was annoyed with him — what did it matter to her. She was thinking of wood paneling and sconces with her coat of arms decorating the great hall.

"There is a question of expenses for all of these improvements of yours," he continued, ignoring her obvious irritation.

She clenched her jaw.

"There will be plenty of money — I shall speak to the King for a loan if things are indeed so desperate."

Margaret would not have tolerated Bishop's beady eyes and impertinent manner except for the fact that her husband had placed him in charge of managing his affairs while he was gone. She had written to him complaining of Bishop many times, but he had never replied to her request.

"We can always sell the lead from some of the old properties to help cover the costs. You must understand that Temple Newsham is to be our family seat. It must be a grand palace. If you cannot comply with my wishes, I shall find someone who can."

"As you wish." He began organizing the papers on the table before them, not meeting her eyes.

She swore she saw him scowl but decided not to comment on it. He bowed as he must do before leaving her presence, but he was markedly cold towards her.

Margaret's eyebrows furrowed as she felt another headache come on. She wished sometimes she was a man who could go out and arrange things for herself rather than rely on men such as Thomas Bishop.

She left her rooms and went to see her son in his little nursery.

The room was kept spotlessly cleaned by a small army of servants. She spared no expense in his care. Besides his wet nurse and rockers, she made sure there was always someone about to care for his needs.

His crib was set close to the fire. The burning apple-wood released a sweet odor in the room. Her eyes swept over the new tapestries hung on the wall to keep the room insulated from the bitter cold outside.

The nurse watching over him stood and curtseyed when she saw her come in.

"How is the Lord Darnley?"

"Sleeping, milady." The nurse smiled down at her young charge. "He looks as peaceful as an angel."

Margaret approached, trying to keep as quiet as possible lest she wake him.

His face was pale and his little dark eyelashes stood out. She noted how his eyes seemed to be moving beneath his eyelids.

"Is he dreaming?"

She placed a tentative hand on his head feeling his forehead for any signs of fever.

"Certainly, he fed well earlier. Now he is probably dreaming of joining his father in Scotland."

Margaret smiled at the thought of him riding beside his father on a large warhorse — their banner flying proudly behind them.

She called for a chair to be brought and sat herself down beside her son, watching him in his sleep. Her mind was thinking of his illustrious future. When he was older, perhaps he could join Prince Edward's household. He was a precious boy — one of only two Tudor boys.

Though she had been excluded from the succession, perhaps her uncle would change his mind as he often did.

Margaret was propped up in her bed, but the soft pillows did nothing to dull the pain. One of her ladies was reading by her side from a selection of hymns. Her voice was grating on her nerves, but she kept herself from complaining. Anne was a good companion, and it wouldn't do to scare her away.

Christina, who was perhaps more perceptive, was stitching a shirt quietly in the corner.

The royal apothecary had sent her more cordials to take. The smell of licorice was enough to make her nauseous now, but she took her medicine dutifully. She had thought her illness was simply due to her pregnancy but it seemed to have persisted.

"Will someone fetch my writing desk?" She could at least be productive while she rested.

"But my lady, the doctor said you should be resting."

"Anne, I cannot sleep anyways. If I don't do something, I fear I shall go quite mad."

She jumped to her feet.

Christina brought the ink and extra parchment.

Margaret settled down to write a message to the King, to thank him for sending his apothecary and to tell him she felt she was improving daily.

She watched as Christina sealed it with wax before setting to work on a letter to her husband.

He was about the King's business. Fighting in his wars to bring the Scots to heel. She did not wish to trouble him with her affairs, but she craved his attention just the same.

She wrote of little Henry growing every day — she

was sure he would start babbling soon. Then told him that she had been ill, though it was nothing serious. Maliciously, Margaret added to her letter how Bishop was failing to listen to her instructions. Hinting perhaps that it was Bishop who had led to this malady in the first place.

She sealed the letter with satisfaction, knowing perhaps that Mathieu would finally dismiss Bishop.

She stayed in bed for the rest of the week, having her chaplain come perform mass for her in the privacy of her rooms.

Despite the reformist views that had taken over the court, she was still a staunch Catholic. Of course, she would never dare openly defy the King. After all, she was currently renovating the home of a staunch Catholic who was beheaded for defending the true faith.

She felt reasonably safe to practice in private in the knowledge that her royal Scottish relations would defend her if it came to that.

Or at least she hoped they would.

It had been long since she spoke to or saw her father, but he would surely not let his only daughter go the scaffold.

She smiled to herself thinking of her darling husband Mathieu who was always trying to persuade her to relinquish her religion.

"I am not as changeable as you are," she said, with fake scorn in her voice.

"I just wish to keep you safe."

"God has kept me safe thus far." She tried reassuring him.

"They warned me you were headstrong." He kissed her brow.

"And yet you still married me. I shall not change now."

He laughed. "No, I cannot see how you would change."

She was pulled out of her thoughts by the appearance of the nurse carrying in her child.

"How is the little lord today?"

"He seems well. A bit pale, perhaps I shall sit with him in the garden."

Margaret was concerned and looked him over. He was pale but his bright eyes were following her gaze, and he even graced her with a little smile.

"It is warm today but do not keep him outdoors for too long."

She didn't want him to catch any evil spirits.

Tomorrow she would join Queen Katherine and her court on their progress, but she loathed to go if Henry was unwell.

She summoned Bishop and told him she planned to delay her departure.

"Milady, the trunks are all packed and ready to go," he argued.

She couldn't believe his impertinence.

"They can wait another day or two."

"The expense and hassle to your household... we have already sent some servants onwards to the court."

"Who is mistress here?" Margaret did not raise her voice, though she was reaching the end of her patience.

He bowed. "I shall ensure everything shall be ready for your departure whenever that shall be."

"Good, and I expect a report on the renovations at Temple Newsham."

He nodded, though it did not escape her notice how he gritted his teeth.

With the King campaigning in France, Queen Katherine was left as regent. She had left on progress fearing the plague in London with the three royal children accompanying her.

It was still a jolly time for the select few invited to join them. They hunted the lush forests during the day and heard lively entertainment in the evening.

Margaret was happy to have the opportunity to see the Lady Mary again.

"Thank you for the lovely brooches you sent me." She was wearing one of the emerald ones.

"I am glad you approved." Mary held her gaze. "You are so blessed to have a son."

Margaret felt the need to cross herself. "I thank God for him every day. You shall have to come meet him soon, when the Queen can spare you."

"I'd be delighted."

"Of course, it would be even better if I could host you at Temple Newsham. Work on the repairs is going poorly, but I fear it is mismanagement rather than... sorry I am rambling. Tell me of yourself." She smiled kindly at the younger woman.

They were near enough in age but Mary's small stature made her forget at times.

"I am often at court these days and back in my father's good graces thanks to the kindness of Queen Katherine."

The two women moved side by side among the hedges of the gardens catching up on news.

When Margaret returned to her rooms that night, she found a letter waiting for her. She broke her husband's seal with exuberance.

*"Dear Meg,*

*I have brilliant news to share with you. I have already written to the King. We have taken Stirling Castle. I am waiting for reinforcements. If we can hold the castle, then I am sure victory is at hand and I can come home to you my sweet.*

*Kiss our son for me and take care of yourself. I cannot dally long but I shall write more to you soon.*

*Your,*

*Mathieu"*

Margaret nearly gave a girlish squeal of glee as she crushed the letter to her chest as if in a hug before kissing his signature.

She had prayed for such a victory. Surely, now her uncle would let her husband come home.

She reread the letter again, noting the haste of his writing in his messy scrawl. She imagined him sitting at his desk scribbling as quickly as he could while his men awaited his commands.

---

September came and the King had returned but her husband had not. His victory had been short lived, his ally had betrayed him and he had to retreat back to Dumbarton. The King was furious and the Scottish lords were becoming intolerant of his presence.

Margaret was back at Stephney Castle, patrolling the rooms in agitation.

Mathieu wrote to her privately of his fears that he was losing support and then he would be left alone. Cornered by his enemies, he would have to face the wolves alone. The King was distracted by his war with France and would not be sending a large army north to Scotland to help him.

Margaret had written a pleading letter to the King to summon back her husband. All she received was a curt reply telling her to stay out of the business of men.

She found she could only scream.

---

The year that had started out with such promise was ending in tragedy, one after another.

Her dear Mathieu was home following in the train of

her uncle, his head down in disgrace after his many failures in Scotland.

As the warm weather gave way to the chill of fall, the Scottish lords sat in parliament and declared her husband a traitor. All his lands and incomes were lost — he was no longer the Earl of Lennox, though he still referred to himself as such.

More than ever they were at the mercy of her uncle.

The English King seemed to like toying with her husband. He liked that more than ever, Lennox had to grovel at his feet. There was nowhere else for him to go.

When her husband visited them at Stephney Castle, he spent most of his time at his writing desk, writing letter after letter to the Scottish Parliament, to his friends, to anyone who might plead his case.

His anxiety made her just as distracted. She had no taste for food, or riding. Nothing could draw a smile from her lips.

Most days she sat before the fire, an unopened book of prayer in her lap. She did not care to mediate the disputes of the tenants on her lands, nor go over the renovations being done at Temple Newsham.

She was utterly distraught. Or she thought she was until the nursemaid came into her room looking pale.

"What is it?"

"My lady, I think you should come. The little lord is unwell — I have asked the Steward to summon the doctor immediately."

Margaret looked at her as though she was speaking in tongues.

"Unwell?" she repeated.

"He has not been eating well but today he has refused everything we have tried to give him and he is running hot." The nurse was studying the floor before her, refusing to look her in the eye.

"Why was I not told?" Margaret jumped to her feet, her heart pounding as she pushed past the useless woman.

She never heard her response as she slammed the door to her solar behind her.

They were crowded around the crib in the nursery — the maids — whispering amongst each other. They stepped aside for her to see her little son. She could see immediately how pale he looked. His once chubby cheeks seemed gaunt.

When she looked up at the women, she could see they had all but pressed themselves against the panels of the wall, wishing to disappear.

"Little Henry, tell your mama what is the matter?" She picked him up. He did feel warm but perhaps this wasn't truly a fever. He was not red or blotchy. There were no signs that this was the sweat. She said a silent prayer of thanks. She cooed at him but he seemed to pay her no attention. His little mouth remained set in a grimace.

Just then her husband entered the nursery, the doctor following close behind him. She all but ran over to them.

"Something is not right." It was all she could say.

Her husband held her as the doctor examined the

small child. By some miracle she had not fainted. The doctor then questioned the maids.

"It might just be a bit of indigestion," he said finally, though Margaret felt his face was too grim for such a simple diagnosis. "I shall make a cordial — mix it with his milk and see if he improves. It will be in God's hands."

Margaret choked back a cry. No.

For three days she sat by his side, and every day she watched him grow weaker and weaker. It was a struggle to feed him. When they managed to coax him to eat, he tended to vomit it up later on.

Mathieu sat with her as often as he could. He was holding her tightly in his arms on the fourth day when he whispered into her hair that they should call for the priest to say the last rites.

"No!"

"My dear, would it not be a mercy for him to die in his faith..."

"He is not to die," she hissed back at him. "He will recover."

"Meg..."

She slumped against him.

By the fifth day, she was dressed in mourning, listening to the priest say the mass over the little coffin draped in black satin.

It was a small affair — no one would travel up the road from London for his funeral. So her young son who had held such a promising future would be buried behind the small chapel in a quiet solemn ceremony.

Later they would erect a small monument in remembrance of him at Temple Newsham. Matthew had promised her this. But in the same breath he reminded her it was important not to dwell on sadness.

There would be others.

Children died all the time.

Margaret knew this as well as anyone else. It was a fact of life, but it was harder to accept when she was going through the loss. Had she not suffered enough?

The King sent a generous offering of clothes for her. Dark blues and blacks. These would be made into mourning clothes for her to wear. Lady Mary wrote to her that she prayed every day for the small soul that had departed this world.

Margaret was comforted that Catholic prayers would be said for her son. In private, she said them also, but Matthew had refused to hear of a Catholic ceremony.

Everything was to be done according to the King's law.

The King was tolerant of Margaret and her barely concealed Catholicism, but her husband did not wish to be so brazenly defiant, knowing that the King burned both Lutherans and Catholics at the stake.

Her husband, as always, bent whichever way the wind blew. She should learn from him but she remained stubborn.

# CHAPTER 2

## 1546

THE CHRISTMAS SEASON passed in relative silence.

Margaret had her steward hand out New Years gifts to their tenants and let him oversee the feast for all those who came to their little castle. She remained sequestered in her rooms or praying in the chapel. Her ladies kept her company, though many of them, tiring of the gloom hanging around her rooms, often snuck out on little errands.

Margaret did not begrudge them their freedom. She had never imagined she would fall into such despair. Only Matthew's presence seemed to lighten her spirits.

He was often called to court now — her uncle was determined to arrange a marriage between the Queen of Scots and his son — uniting England and Scotland into one formidable land. It seemed that once the roads were passable, Matthew would be sent back to Scotland to negotiate with the Scots lords.

For once she found herself wishing that winter would

never subside. She clung desperately to him and often pulled him to her bed. They never spoke of it but she was desperate to conceive again. Margaret wished to find a way to fill the emptiness that Henry had left in her heart.

More than that she needed to feel loved and adored. She found it hard to sleep if Matthew's arms were not around her frame, holding her tightly.

"Are you not afraid to return?" She pressed him when he came to visit her bed chamber one night, a mug of hot ale in his hands.

"It is my duty to go to Scotland. If I refuse, I shall appear defeated for certain. Besides this is the only way we shall recoup my title and lands."

She waved him off. "The King provides us with everything we need."

"He is very generous." Matthew set down the mug by her bedside. "But it is still charity. I would have what is rightfully ours returned to us. Then we would not be beggars. I see how the English lords look at me. I do not command respect."

Margaret did not point out that, as the niece of a King, she was entitled to the money he gave her. It was not charity from her point of view, but her husband was proud. As her husband, he should automatically have the respect of nobles.

"Then do not go to court or Scotland. Stay here with me. I am told Temple Newsham will be livable in the spring and we should move there together."

He smiled at her patting her shoulder.

"I am being serious."

"When you pout like that I am reminded of our early carefree days of marriage."

She swatted his hand away from her but at the same time beckoned him to sit beside her on the bed.

"I shall not be gone long — these negotiations cannot last too long. The Scots will either capitulate to the King's demands or they will reject him and there is nothing we can do."

"Which do you think is more likely to happen?"

"I shall do my best to see the King's demands will be accomplished."

So he thought he had little chance of success. Was he doomed to be the scapegoat yet again?

---

"Call for Sir Alsopp," Margaret said wearily from her bed.

She was feeling unwell again this morning. Her back ached and her head was pounding. She was sure the doctor would be able to help her with her ailments.

"Right away." Her secretary bowed, leaving the room.

One of her ladies replaced the cool compress on her forehead. It brought her temporary relief.

"Has there been no word from my husband?"

"There has been no messenger."

"None would dare risk the long journey from Scotland in this weather."

Margaret glared at her unhelpful lady.

She bit her lip to refrain from complaining out loud

that he had promised her to write often and return to her before the end of March.

They were to move in April and she needed him.

"Would you like to take some broth?"

Margaret shook her head. Even light broth was beyond her at the moment.

In due course, the doctor arrived with his medicine bag filled with cures and tinctures. He spent a good portion of the morning going over her symptoms and examining her urine. He suggested a course of leeches and promised he would make her a poultice for her back.

"Your humors are simply in disarray." He smiled down at her in a manner meant to be reassuring. "But it is nothing to fear. I shall have you well again."

The leeches left her skin looking as pale as the snow outside but the plasters on her back seemed to alleviate some of the pain she felt, and she was able to take a seat by the window during the day.

Her appetite still had not recovered, and it was not until her ladies commented that perhaps there was another cause for her feeling ill that she was suddenly struck with a happy thought.

She had missed her course.

It was early but perhaps there was new life growing in her womb.

Margaret knew the wise thing to do would be to wait, but she called for her writing desk and penned a quick scribbled note to her husband. Perhaps it would urge him to conclude the business in Scotland faster.

Just as her messenger was sent out riding down the

cobblestone road north, another was riding up from the south. Margaret vaguely recognized the man as one of Queen Katherine's distant relatives — a second cousin perhaps — that she had taken into her service as a page.

"A letter from the Queen for you, my lady." He pulled out a sealed letter from his jerkin.

"You have ridden in much haste, why don't you go to the kitchens and help yourself to some food while I read my letter." Margaret's fingers skimmed over the seal checking to see if it was still intact.

Spies often resealed letters.

"I was commanded to stay with you while you read and see to it that the letter was disposed of after," he all but whispered.

Margaret was alert at once. She nodded in reply and then broke the seal in one swift practiced motion. There was no mistaking the Queen's handwriting. If she had taken so much trouble to write, this must be a matter of much importance.

Her eyes scanned the letter and she had to fight to keep her face impassive. Her ladies in waiting were sitting by the fire far away from her, but that didn't mean they weren't watching her.

*Dearest Lady Margaret,*

*I hope this letter finds you well. You have always been a loyal friend to myself and the King, your uncle. I will be blunt — I find I am losing my friends. They are slipping away from my rooms and there are rumors that my enemies are moving against me. You can only imagine how much this grieves me.*

*I have only ever been a loyal servant of my husband the King and wish only to serve him and this country to the best of my ability. Bishop Gardiner is keen on finding me guilty of some heresy he perceives I have committed. I swear to you that I have done nothing against the King's and God's laws. I fear he wishes to push the King back into the arms of the Pope and he shall sacrifice me to do it. I pray you shall remain my loyal friend. I invite you to join me at court at your leisure. I fear your uncle is being kept away from those who wish to council him.*

*I also wish to warn you that you are likely to be watched. Gardiner will stop at nothing to purge the court of those he sees as his enemies. He is jealous of your husband and the preference the King has towards you. I feel you should know that your husband's secretary, Thomas Bishop, has been to court often and though he mainly reports to the King news from Scotland, I also know that he is often sequestered with the Bishop for private meetings. I do not know what he says but it cannot be good.*

*Come to court as soon as you can.*

*Your friend,*

*K*

Margaret crushed the parchment in her hands. She threw it into a nearby blazer and watched it turn to black soot.

"You may tell your mistress that I shall come to court as soon as I am able. Feel free to rest and eat in my hall." She dismissed him.

Once he was gone, she paced the length of her rooms, ignoring the stares of her ladies.

Intrigue had found its way into her life once more. She was not eager to jump back into the fray of court life. A hand rested on her stomach that was still flat. What else could she do though?

This wasn't just about the Queen. She had seen many Queens come and go and had been helpless to stop their demise, but if Katherine was correct then whether she wanted to or not she was already being dragged into whatever conspiracy was brewing. Once again she cursed Thomas Bishop and his meddling. She had no proof of his ill-doing but there was no doubt in her mind that he was up to no good.

She refused to be dragged down without a fight.

She stewed in her anger and fear all afternoon before finally deciding that, after she oversaw the household move to Temple Newsham, she would go to court by May.

She had hoped to establish their country seat and settle down to prepare for the birth of her new baby, if there indeed was one, but there was no time to rest. Besides, if she was at court, she was more likely to hear news of her husband faster.

She rode with a huge escort of men flanking her on the road. Her goods had traveled ahead of her in wagons pulled by oxen. Margaret was bundled up in a litter, as her condition did not permit her to ride. It was still early days, but she did not wish to risk anything going wrong.

They tried to play at cards, but the roads were so uneven that it made the task impossible.

They were on the road for several days and they had to stay the night at various houses along the way. Sometimes there was no room for her whole escort to be housed, and they had to find lodgings in barns and cottages of tenants nearby. The great monasteries were torn down and could no longer shelter travelers.

Margaret was surprised when she was not led to her usual rooms at Hampton Court. She did not let her feelings show on her face.

Even so, the steward felt it necessary to make some excuse about the excess of visitors to court and said the King would have her every comfort met.

She would put this to rights, but first she had to rest.

The journey from Temple Newsham had been long and arduous. Already she missed her new rooms in the south wing — the bed was soft and the room meticulously decorated with her favorite tapestries. She had picked the rooms to be dark in the morning and have the sun shining through in the afternoon, so she could sleep in longer if she desired. From her window, she could see the pond where Mathieu promised he would buy a pair of swans to paddle around for her pleasure. She knew that he would also fill the pond with fish.

He was practical, unlike herself, and would never build anything for the mere sake of pleasure, but he had been born and raised in the wilds of Scotland — even his time in France had not dampened the lessons of his childhood.

Margaret found him endearing and she wouldn't begrudge him a few fish. He did not want their country house to be a mere representation of their wealth and station, he wanted it to be a productive, profitable house.

Her mind was on making the house comfortable for herself and their new child. She imagined that the King might travel on progress to her house as well, and she would be immensely proud if she could house the court in comfort and ease.

The rooms she was in now felt drafty and she ordered a large fire to be built.

By the time Mathieu came to see how she was settling in, he found that she was busy ordering the servants to rearrange the furniture and calling for furs and tapestries she had brought with her to be hung on the walls.

"What is this, dearest Meg?" he said, walking in with a smile. "Are you not content with remodeling our home?"

She greeted him sweetly. "I have not failed to notice we are not in our usual rooms, but I shall make us comfortable regardless."

His smile faltered. "It does not matter. There are so many people come to court this season we are lucky that we do not have to find shelter in the city."

Margaret did not wish to complain further in front of the listening servants, who were bound to gossip or report what she said.

"Of course, my lord."

"And are you feeling well? Not too exhausted from the journey?" He took a seat beside her on the couch his gaze drifting to her belly.

"As good as can be expected — I am glad we had good weather."

"I am glad you shall be at court, where you shall have access to the best midwives and doctors." She smiled but couldn't help but notice his grave expression.

"What troubles you?" she asked, her voice barely a whisper as she leaned her head against his shoulder.

"I do not—" He took a long pause, as if trying to collect his thoughts. "I have hopes that this campaign season will be better, but I fear that the allies I am counting on will fail to materialize. You must speak of this to no one. Margaret, it is important."

Margaret nodded in agreement. She rested her hand on his chest.

"You are a great commander. This time you are sure to succeed. We will be in favor once again."

"It is not merely the King's favor I seek. I want my lands restored to me."

She nodded. It did not much matter to her one way or another as long as she had her houses and living paid for. She would pray for the soul of the little one growing now in her belly that he would be strong and thrive.

A few years ago, she would have gone on pilgrimage

to Our Lady of Walsingham, but such places were torn down now. There were no shrines to visit. No holy places where miracles occurred. This was a new England. A country where Catholics were burned alongside heretics. The King decided what was heresy now — he often changed his mind from one day to the next.

Margaret knew that Matthew thought she was being foolish hiring a Catholic priest to be her private chaplain. But she heard mass in secret and outwardly she conformed as best she could. In a way, she felt safe in the knowledge that she was the King's beloved niece, and in the past, she had also enjoyed the distant support of her mother, the Queen of Scots.

The King was a harsher man these days, and she should remember that.

At length, she was settled in and she joined the Queen in her rooms. It was a much more subdued place than it had been the last time she had been here. Gone were the scholars lecturing to the ladies, and the printers with their new books. Instead Queen Katherine and her ladies were sitting around sewing shirts to donate to the poor.

They seemed to be trying to emulate the very definition of wifely bliss. However, a veteran courtier like herself could never be fooled. Margaret could feel the tension flowing through the room like the dangerous undercurrent of a quiet sea.

Margaret performed her elegant curtsey for the

Queen, who smiled warmly at her and hugged her tightly.

"You are welcome back to court," she said. "Condolences for your loss."

Margaret had to fight to suppress the fresh stab of pain that threatened to overwhelm her.

"Thank you, your grace." She moved to take a seat beside the King's daughter, the Lady Mary, who squeezed her hand to reassure her.

They had never been the closest of friends but they had both faced the King's cruelty and imprisonment. They had survived by complying to his every demand, begging for forgiveness though they knew each word they spoke was false. So now here they both were, hiding their true beliefs from him. To say it had created a strong bond between them would be an understatement.

There was little talk among the ladies other than discussing the days hunting and how handsome the King had looked in his new coat. Though in truth, most of their eyes had been fixed on Thomas Seymour, recently returned from his adventures on the open seas. His dark beauty catching the eye of every lady.

Margaret, who was pregnant, could not ride out with them and had nothing to contribute to the conversation. She felt the pang of being on the outside looking in, but she would not trade her condition for the world.

"Shall you miss your husband when he leaves for Scotland?" Lady Anne Hastings asked.

"Of course, I shall." Margaret frowned at the rude question.

"My husband thinks he is incapable of capturing the regent and taking power in Scotland. He is wasting English money and men, but I suppose as a Scotsman himself he does not particularly care."

"My husband is a loyal Englishman. The King himself trusted him with this task."

"Has he not already failed to achieve what the King demanded of him? Perhaps he is merely incompetent."

The Queen interceded before they came to blows. "This is hardly a proper discussion to be holding now," she said, fixing them both in turn with a cold stare.

Margaret tried to calm herself — there was no point getting herself riled up, besides it might harm the baby.

"There is bad blood between your husband and hers," Mary explained under her breath.

"Apparently," Margaret seethed. "How dare she speak out like this to me? In public, no less."

Mary shook her head. She did not know.

"Is the King angry with me?" Margaret asked, her voice barely a whisper, thinking back to her subpar rooms.

"He does not speak to me of such things." Mary shrugged. "He has been...frustrated lately, though we do not know with what. I am afraid the pain in his leg troubles him."

She spoke carefully, in case anyone overheard her commenting on the King's health.

"Well I hope I have done nothing to invoke his displeasure." Margaret looked towards the Queen. "Is he happy with her?" It seemed like such an odd question. Would this sixth wife finally be able to please her uncle at last? Or would he find a reason to cast her aside as well?

Or, even worse, had he already?

"Bishop Gardiner is always by his side, helping him with the pain in his leg." Mary looked around the room as she spoke. "He would influence the King to return to the old ways — he is a brave holy man. Unfortunately, those who hold with the reforms are out of favor."

Margaret knew exactly what she was implying. So the Queen and her kin were out of favor. When the King had first married her, everyone had feared that she was a papist, but in fact, the opposite proved to be true. She proved to have a love of learning and she had come under the influence of Bishop Cranmer — the old Boleyn Champlain who everyone knew was a secret Lutheran. Her views proved to stop short of what many would call heretical.

Even so, Margaret had liked her. She was not so religious that she would avoid her company. Besides, the King had seemed to encourage her learning. At least at first.

She wondered what had happened. The Queen had been a good stepmother to his children and a loyal companion, from what she could tell. She wondered if the King was annoyed she was not with child, but what could he seriously expect with his infirmities. It was an open secret that he had been impotent for quite some time.

Not even young Katherine Howard had been able to conceive.

In any case, this did not help Margaret understand why she was out of favor if it was the papists who held the King's ear. The King knew where her true beliefs lay, her star should be rising not falling.

No, something else must have happened.

She hoped it wasn't her husband's failures that had led to this decline of his estimation of hers. After all, she relied on everything from her uncle. Ever since her mother had all but abandoned her in England. Though she would not have traded living in England for Scotland for anything. When she thought of the wild lawless place, she would say a silent prayer of thanks for her good fortune.

Her silent contemplation did not go unnoticed.

"Perhaps you would enjoy a walk through the gardens. You are looking quite pale," Mary commented.

"There is a chill in the wind today," the Queen interceded, having heard what she said. "But I can send for the doctor to prescribe a draft for you if you prefer."

"Thank you for your concern." Margaret smiled at both women. "I was merely far away in my thoughts."

The rest of the Queen's ladies seemed to have taken up the mantle and began offering her advice, though many were unmarried or had not carried a child in their belly. But with little else to entertain them, they decided to play nurse to Margaret.

She couldn't help but glow under their kind ministrations and advice. She had been away in the country for too long, isolated with the busy work of keeping a household running and mourning her loss. These women would never understand the pain she felt, but she appreciated the company of her equals — even the snooty glare of Lady Anne Hastings.

Mary invited her to share a cup of ale in her rooms and the two of them retired long before the others had gone to bed.

"My husband brought me here to be cared for, and it seems I am to be spoiled with attention." Margaret laughed, throwing her feet up on a cushion. They were throbbing from her being on her feet all day and then sitting upright.

"He is a most caring husband to not have left you alone," Lady Mary agreed.

Margaret studied her cousin, so close in age to herself. She should have been married a long time ago. The faint lines on her face indicated she needed some love and care herself.

"But I am selfish — you look as though you need some pampering yourself."

"It is true." Mary nodded. "Perhaps when the court goes on progress, I shall retire to my own estates to rest."

"There are plans to travel?" Margaret sipped at the steaming cup of mulled ale in her hands. The familiar scent of spices calming her stomach. She thought of her uncle who could barely walk on his own any more. How did he take the strain of riding from house to house all over the country?

"Nothing is certain, though my father, the King, speaks of it."

Wishful thinking more like, but Margaret kept this dangerous thought to herself.

"I myself hope that the court will not travel far this summer." She placed a hand on her belly. "I shall not be in any state to move around."

Mary smiled kindly. "I pray for your safe deliverance every night. I cannot wait to see this new babe of yours."

"I pray as well." Margaret sighed. "I also pray that my husband will have returned to me by then."

Mary patted her arm. "I am sure he would not be parted from you a day longer than necessary. His love for you is evident."

Margaret couldn't manage much of a smile. "It is a shame I miss him so much since we seem doomed to be parted often."

She had no doubt that even if he was victorious on his return, her uncle would find some other task that would have him sent away again.

---

It had been a few days since her return to court. Her uncle had been conspicuous in avoiding her. He had greeted her with a stark coldness she had never experienced before. The moment had been laden with tension and made her suspect all the more that something was wrong.

Her husband was too busy with his correspondences

from Scotland — loyal lords who pledged their help when he came at the head of yet another army. There were also more men to hire and provide them with weapons and armor for the fight ahead. All this Mathieu had to present to the King's privy council for their approval.

He rarely spared a moment to see her these days. She could tell that he too was afraid of what would happen should he fail. In the middle of the night, he would sometimes awake in a cold sweat, and Margaret would send for some hot wine to soothe his troubled mind.

She was heading to the Queen's room with her own ladies in waiting after hearing Katherine had returned from a ride when she decided to take a detour. She knew that Matthew had a private audience with the King today to discuss battle plans. He had left their rooms with his secretary trailing after him, laden with papers and maps.

The chamber outside the King's inner sanctum was a busy place. Besides his household staff and clerks waiting to be called in to serve him, there was a healthy amount of courtiers waiting for their chance to be in his presence.

A chance to speak to the King meant more to these men than the fresh clean air outside. A word from the King could overturn fortunes in an instant.

A quick scan of the room told her that her husband was no longer waiting here — perhaps he was inside or had retreated back to their rooms already. She had been midway to turning for the entry when she spotted someone that made her stop short.

There among the darkly clothed clerks was Thomas Bishop. His unkempt hair marking him out among his well groomed peers. The sneer on his face sent a burst of fury racing through her veins. The nerve of this man, who was he to sneer at her?

She did not give him the satisfaction of her attention for a moment longer. Margaret marched out of the chamber, her long strides made her ladies have to hurry to catch up to her.

"My lady, are you alright?" Martha, the newest addition to her retinue, asked.

"Quite well, thank you." She knew her curt reply spoke otherwise. "Send a message to my husband that I wish to speak to him when he can spare a moment of his time."

"Of course." The lady curtseyed and ran off.

No doubt she would stop somewhere along the way to meet with the young gentleman who had caught her eye and was sending her love poems. Margaret tolerated such behavior as long as this game of love did not go too far.

She had been young and reckless once too. Her games had ended with her imprisonment though. Perhaps she would have a word with her tonight. Her father had entrusted her into her keeping. It would not do to have her reputation sullied because of her neglect.

---

"What is it, sweetheart?" Matthew found her later that evening. He had dined with the King privately and had not gotten away.

"Thomas Bishop is here," she huffed. When he did not seem surprised she continued. "Well, how can you be so calm? He's out for revenge."

Matthew laughed at that, which put her in an even worse mood. Seeing her scowl he rushed to console her.

"No." She pushed him away, though her attempt was half-heartened. "Listen to me. Isn't it convenient that his appearance at court might be why we are not given our usual rooms? And why my uncle seems so displeased with me?"

"Don't you think you are exaggerating?"

"Who knows what lies he has whispered in his ear!"

"Calm yourself or I shall not listen to you." Matthew placed a hand on her belly. "Think of this little one. Is the elegance of a room so important to you?"

"No, of course not." Margaret took a few deep breaths to steady herself. "It does not mean it is not important. The King is changed lately. I would not have him angered with us, and he grows distrustful. If that man poisoned him against us, I fear for us."

"Why would he do such a thing?"

"We dismissed him from our service, did we not? I constantly fought with him."

He smiled. "I remember your fights. Perhaps you should learn to treat those who work for us with a touch more kindness."

"You are not taking me seriously."

Matthew shook his head. "I am sorry. It is hard for me to not smile at my haughty wife growing big with our

ANNE R BAILEY

child trying to bring the roof down over our heads with her conspiracy theories."

"There has been nothing in my life except conspiracies."

He pulled her close to him. "Nothing else?"

She grinned now hearing the heat in his voice. "Well, perhaps something else too. But you shall not distract me. I have been thinking about this all day."

"Then you have too much time on your hands if you have been dwelling on this for so long." He kissed her forehead as he often did. "Request an audience with your uncle if you have to. If Thomas Bishop has indeed been trying to stir up trouble between you, then do your best to put his mind to rest. But remember he is probably here seeking employment."

"Hardly, that man is up to something."

"Come to bed, I am tired and would enjoy your company. Before long, I shall lose you as my bedfellow and I shall have nothing but your letters to keep me company in the cold Scottish nights."

Margaret sighed, sad to be reminded of his imminent departure. How many days would she have left? They were simply waiting for the weather to turn before sailing away to war. He was right — she should not trouble him with this now on the eve of his departure.

---

It was an odd thing to request a meeting with her own uncle. A year ago, she would have simply walked up to him when he visited the Queen's rooms, but now she found herself unable to do so.

His eagerness to ignore her took away her bravery. Instead, she approached the Queen to speak to him on her behalf.

"I hope his majesty would spare me a moment of his time," she began her pretty prepared speech. She tried hard to not let it show how much she was irked by having to pay the supplicant.

"I shall speak to him." Katherine was not unkind. "He has neglected his family in favor of his stately duties. Perhaps I shall arrange a musical evening for us all. Prince Edward is to join us in the next week or so — it would be the perfect excuse to pull him away."

A private evening would be wonderful. It wasn't exactly the privacy Margaret had hoped for, but she could not complain either.

---

She was accompanied by her ladies to the docks to see her husband embark on yet another journey to Scotland. Margaret was beginning to think of them as fruitless journeys.

But this time would be different.

For the occasion, she wore a luxurious silver gown, with a red shawl tied around her neck to protect her from the cold. She was the embodiment of the family crest. She gave Matthew her blessing and tried to hold back her tears before the men and ladies watching.

"Be safe, my love," she whispered.

He gave her a hearty kiss to the cheers of his men on board.

"And you as well." He placed a hand on her belly once more.

Margaret wondered if he would return in time for the birth — or if he would return at all. The thought sent a shiver of fear racing down her spine and it took all her courage to keep standing straight, a bright smile plastered on her face.

She had thought about asking him to reconsider going but stopped herself from even asking him to think about it. After all, that would mean she was doubting the prowess of her husband.

His back was straight as he walked up the gangplank, his gait made him look as though he was almost skipping with excitement.

They were both actors in this masque before the court and the soldiers. Neither of them was as confident and fearless as they seemed.

As the ship pulled away from shore, Margaret said a silent prayer. There was no way he would not return to her. She did not know what rankled her spirits so much — she who had been so confident in always getting her way.

She would have to press ahead. There was no other way. While Matthew would battle in Scotland, she would wage her own war here in England.

A war for the King's favor.

# CHAPTER 3

1546-1547

QUEEN KATHERINE HAD ARRANGED for a splendid evening of entertainment. As always, there was masquing, music and even a reading of poetry. The food was brought up from the kitchens in droves for the King, unable to dance, took to eating.

Margaret took her chance as the Queen began dancing for her husband with one of her ladies.

"Your majesty, my dearest uncle," she began, curt-seying low. "I beg for a moment of your time."

She could feel his piercing gaze upon her, but she did not move an inch nor look him in the eye.

"Speak, Lady Lennox. What would you have from me?" he asked, almost begrudgingly, as he all but shoveled another slice of pie in his mouth.

"I would know what it is that I have done to have displeased you so much," she said deciding that being candid with him was the best approach.

He chuckled. "Why would you say I am displeased

ANNE R BAILEY

with you?" She saw he was no longer watching her but staring out at the dancers.

This was an invitation to admit guilt. That was dangerous. Margaret considered her words carefully.

"I could not help but notice that my presence did not give you the pleasure it once did, my lord. If I am a burden upon your court, I will take myself away from here in a moment."

As Margaret spoke, she prayed that she had not invited more trouble upon herself. She was too far gone to comfortably travel in her pregnancy. Although had her mother not fled Scotland heavily pregnant with her in her belly?

He turned his gaze back to her, studying the sincerity of her words.

"I hear troubling reports..." He paused as if for dramatic effect. "...did you know that one of my bitches tried to nip me the other day?"

She shook her head. No.

"I ran her through with my sword." He brandished his dinner knife like a sword and made a slicing motion. "I have no time for troublesome women."

Margaret thought of the little Catherine Howard sent to the block just years ago. It was rumored the King had wanted to kill her himself and only his councilors had stopped him from doing so.

"I would never wish to be a source of trouble for you," she spoke sweetly. "You have always been my protector and benefactor. Though I admit I have not always been deserving of the love you have shown me."

"Hmm."

"I would also hope that you would let me explain myself to you, for everything I have always done has been to gain your favor." This was not a lie, though on occasion she had deviated from her path.

Perhaps he could see how she squirmed uncomfortably or perhaps he was reminded of his love for her because he invited her to stand.

"There are those who speak out against you." He pulled a leg off a roasted quail. "I would have these matters investigated. But I can see you are repentant, and if you are as innocent as you seem, then there is no reason why I cannot welcome you into my good graces again."

Margaret gave him one of her best smiles, a hand moving to her expanding belly.

He caught the motion and then looked back to the Queen, dancing light-footed among her ladies. Even though she was fast approaching middle age she was still beautiful, especially now as her cheeks turned rosy red with the exertion of dancing.

"And the Queen? Do you think the Queen may yet conceive?" he asked, almost as though they were both conspirators whispering behind closed doors.

"We all pray she does soon. Prince Edward would love a brother to play with." She looked over to the blonde little boy perched upon his own seat under a canopy of estate.

"Yes, yes." The King waved his hands indicating he tired of the conversation. A new plate arrived at his table, mutton in a thick gravy. She curtseyed to him three times as she retreated from his side.

She found herself a seat and watched the festivities, her feet tapping along to the music. Her mood altogether lifted. If the King was willing to listen to her, then all was not lost.

---

She had spent a large portion of her morning going through her chests of clothing and thinking of what she would wear. Her maids were exhausted from pulling out dress after dress, but she could not settle on one.

Finally, she chose a gown of dark green with a gold girdle tied around her waist. Margaret felt that she looked regal without being ostentatious. A subtle reminder to her uncle of their family ties.

Today, she would do her best to placate him. If only she knew exactly what he was upset about or what that little snake, Rich, had told him; then she would be able to prepare a proper defense.

At length she headed towards the King's privy chambers. She could not stroll past the guards, though she saw many an old friend do that very thing. She waited patiently among all the other supplicants knowing that he would summon her when he was ready.

It was Bishop Gardiner who caught her eye when he strode through the shut wooden doors.

"Lady Margaret, the King will see you now."

Her eyebrow rose out of surprise — she was surprised he was being used as an errand boy.

He must have caught the look, for he smiled and offered her his arm. "I thought it would be nice for you to see a friendly face."

She wondered what conspiracy she had been dragged into.

The King was seated in his large wooden chair placed in front of the fire. It cast eerie shadows on his face that created an ominous feeling in her gut. She curtseyed to him three times and came up smiling her most genuine of smiles.

"Well, now that you are here. What have you to say? Nothing to confess?" He grabbed a goblet of wine and motioned for a page to bring him a plate of sweetmeats.

"I have nothing to confess. At least, I do not know in what way I have offended your majesty," she corrected herself.

Gardiner was no longer by her side. He had taken a seat on a stool — not too close or too far, she noticed, as she waited for her uncle's response.

"Some have accused you of being a papist." His eyes seemed to glint and her stomach churned with nausea.

"I follow the Church of England and worship as you have instructed us to." She knew she was sounding defensive and that was a sign of weakness. "You are the head of the Church of England."

This was not a lie, though she did not believe it herself.

"Have you not paid for chantry priests? With money I have given you?"

Margaret bit the inside of cheek tasting blood. "I did not know this was not allowed."

"It is nothing but a silly superstition." His words were cold.

"I-it was f-for my son," she stammered. "You had paid for Queen Jane to have priests..."

He slammed his fist on the table before him. The sound ricocheted through the silent room.

"I did not know you had outlawed this practice," she repeated firmly. "I was mourning for my son."

She would not be more apologetic than that. The accusation had stung; she couldn't believe she was here, accused of something that was so commonplace.

"Your Grace, Lady Margaret should be forgiven. She was distraught and her husband was not by her side to guide her." Bishop Gardiner spoke up.

She could have kissed him out of sheer gratefulness.

"You would defend her actions?" the King smirked knowingly. "I know which way you lean, I shouldn't be surprised."

"As your loyal servant, I merely want to make you aware of the facts," he said, his head bowed.

"And the other matter. The money from the selling of lead roofs?" The King turned his attention back to her. "How do you account for this?"

"Merely, to say that I had indeed ordered the sale of the lead roofs, but I have used it to repair and renovate Temple Newsham. I was unaware I had done anything wrong. I wanted to make it a fit place should your grace ever choose to visit us."

"Every time I accuse anyone of anything, all I hear is that I am innocent or I did not know." He waved his large hands. "I shall ask for your chamberlain to send me a record of your accounts."

"I shall provide you with whatever you require."

"I require loyalty and absolute obedience."

"And you have it. Of course you have it."

"We shall see. If what you say is true then we shall be perfect friends again."

She knew what would happen if he found anything he disapproved of.

She returned to her rooms feeling lightheaded. Her nausea made her unable to eat dinner, though she had some broth prepared for her before she retired for bed. No one asked where she had been, but they assumed that her interview with the King had gone well enough since she was not yet again imprisoned.

With the onset of summer — all trouble seemed to be forgotten or, at the very least, the King could not find any concrete proof against her.

She had made some headway, too, in complaining of the arrogance of Thomas Rich and how he believed he was superior to them all despite his low birth. That reminded the King all too much of Cardinal Wolsey, and it did not sit well with him. Soon Rich was no longer lurking around court — he had found some employment elsewhere, seeing that he had failed to sway the King.

Margaret knew the victory was an empty one. There

would always be those looking to make a rift between her and her uncle — if only to stir up trouble. In the end she had lost, for now she no longer had the knowledge that prayers were being sung for her son's soul.

There was nothing to be done about it now, except hope in her heart that the King would change his mind.

Her growing belly added to her distraction and the news that the King of France was sending a new ambassador. Suddenly they were to transform into a lively court, spilling over with abundant wealth.

The Queen was busy organizing her ladies to throw on a pageant, and the great nobles of the land assembled at court with their ladies.

Anne of Cleves appeared from Richmond, bedecked in rich clothes fine enough for the Queen. Margaret's eyes scanned her up and down from the fine cut of her cloth to the expensive jewels she wore. She noted with silent satisfaction that at least she had remained slimmer than this woman despite her pregnancy.

At first, Anne had plumped up pleasantly, but it seemed that she had no intention of stopping, and she appeared to have an ever widening girth. She had never been a petite woman, but now, after a few years in England, she seemed to have ballooned. She was not ugly but no one could doubt now why the King had put her aside. Queen Katherine would not have anything to fear from her.

The two women greeted each other cordially. The new wife and the former — the courtiers were ready with comparisons and comments. Ready like hungry hounds for any scent of gossip.

Well they were doomed to be disappointed.

The Lady Elizabeth arrived as well and the court seemed to swell even more.

There was no doubt as to whose daughter she was as she strode through Greenwich as though she belonged there. One would never know she was the castoff daughter of the King's second wife. Though as the marriage was annulled, she was technically a bastard. Officially, she was third in line for the throne.

It was not long before a page came riding up to the palace to warn everyone that the Admiral was on his way — the welcoming party escorting him from his ship. Margaret had refused to ride in her condition, and so she waited with the Queen at Greenwich for the King and Admiral to arrive.

With a collective intake of breath, they sprang into action. Last minute touches were put on the cakes and pies to be served, the wine decanted, musicians tuned their instruments. Margaret watched this all from her spot behind the Queen, sitting regally on her throne — a throne occupied by so many before her.

A few stragglers appeared, rushing through side entrances just as the trumpets outside the great hall blared.

Dressed in their finery, the players took up their parts as the Admiral of France, Claude d'Annebaut, appeared. He entered a step behind the King of England, dressed in pale blue silk. A smile ready on his lips.

He bowed low before the Queen, sweeping off his hat. Margaret heard him whisper "enchante" as he kissed her outstretched hand. Queen Katherine greeted him warmly, though pulled her hand away quickly, her eyes fixed on her husband.

Margaret wondered if it was for reassurance or to make sure he saw that she did not care for this bold man.

"You are most welcome. Please have a seat — I hope the journey across the channel was not overly tiresome."

"Of course not, but my spirits are lifted to be among such beautiful ladies." He looked past the Queen and winked at the ladies in waiting.

He was charming — as were all French men it seemed — possessing a self-assured quality that put everyone at ease. They danced for him and entertained him with tales.

Whether they knew it or not, the ladies gravitated towards him as though he were their trusted confidant.

The King of France had chosen well. Here was someone who could negotiate peace.

Margaret thought of her husband struggling in Scotland — perhaps without French support the Scots would come to heel.

The royal retinue left Greenwich traveling through the streets of London to Hampton Court.

The streets they had passed through had been ordered to be cleared, so most of the foul-smelling refuse was cleared out of the way. People crowded around to catch a glimpse of the court on the move but were not in the way, slowing their path.

Like their performance the night before, this was simply a masque.

The ambassador was never short of compliments for what he saw. Margaret was amused — one would think he was ready to cast aside his allegiance to the French crown and declare for England. But this was all a game. Just as they pretended that Henry was still the most handsome King in Christendom, they now pretended they were a land of wealth and prosperity.

At Hampton Court, the King awaited them with a grand feast.

He presented the ambassador with a gold chain studded with jet black stones. In return, the ambassador presented him with a beautiful sword from the King of France. To the Queen who was well known for liking exotic birds, a beautiful white parrot was brought out. Even Margaret, who was more annoyed by the squawking birds, was impressed.

After the festivities of the ambassador's arrival, Margaret had time to herself. She craved for news from her husband but he had remained silent.

The campaign must not be going well.

She knew it in her heart, though she tried to be optimistic. She hoped this would be the last time he would be sent — the last time she would have to face the loneliness and uncertainty of separation. In the end, she had her secretary inquire around from the lord privy seal if there was any news from Scotland.

The King was receiving several dispatches a week,

but besides knowing her husband still lived, she did not learn anything more substantial.

In the worry for her husband, she did not catch the subtle shift in the current of the court. With the French Ambassador's departure, the court moved to Windsor but the King had fallen ill and was secluded in his rooms. Any plans for a summer progress were quietly dropped.

There seemed to be no concern in the Queen's rooms, and she went about as normal though she sent frequent missives to her ailing husband. During his previous illnesses, he had called for her to sit by his side, but now he had sent her away.

"He wishes for me to look after the children and the court," Queen Katherine had informed them after one of her requests to see him was denied.

All her ladies nodded as if she had not been making excuses.

Later in the evening, Margaret watched her feed the note she received from the King's page into flames.

The next day, Lady Anne was absent from the Queen's rooms. Margaret walked around with pursed lips wondering what trouble was afoot. Her ever expanding belly was causing her discomfort as she walked behind the Queen in her train, but at least her morning sickness had abated.

She did not have any confidants among the ladies of this court now that Lady Mary had retreated to her country house. The official excuse had been that she needed a reprieve from the heat of London but now Margaret had her doubts.

By dinner she heard that Lady Anne was taken in for questioning. Looking at the Queen more carefully, it was undeniable how she looked paler than usual and her ready smile gone from her face. She looked more matronly than ever.

Margaret was at a loss for what she should do. She should leave for Temple Newsham, but she was equally worried about appearing rude and she had promised her husband she would stay in the care of the King.

Two days later, Margaret returned to her rooms after dinner to find they had been searched. Her maid servant frantically grumbling about rude guards as she was tidying away the things. Sheets and clothes would have to be refolded in their chests.

A quick scan of the room told Margaret that her books had been taken away and her writing desk had been rifled through. She bit the inside of her cheek. There was nothing she was hiding, she was sure they would find nothing to accuse her of any crime. Still, she couldn't keep her heart from racing at the knowledge that the shadow of suspicion had fallen on her as well.

The King recovered but the spirits of the court are not lifted.

As he dined, he glared about the court and at the Queen, despite her pleasant conversation. When she arranged for a troupe of performers to put on a play for him, he did not even crack a smile, though they did their job very well. Margaret watched all of this, wishing more and more to disappear.

Over and over, he reached for the plates of food —

everyone was full, but rather than risking offending him, they all decided to pick at the food in front of them, pretending to eat. Margaret had been pretending for years; she knew how to pace herself but the stress and pregnancy were not helping her stomach.

It was clear by the end of the following week that the Queen was being investigated.

Everyone had their own theories but it seemed the King had settled on heresy. She was a reformer at heart — everyone knew this even though she had been raised a Catholic and was married to one of the staunchest practicing Catholics for several years.

Margaret would rather not debate that the King's way was also heretical — the Pope was the head of the church, but she would not voice this opinion out loud. Not now.

When a letter arrived from Lady Mary, she could not help but tear the seal, eager to see the contents of the letter. A quick scan told her that she was invited to Hudson to visit her cousin. She said a silent prayer of thanks for this excuse to leave. Now she won't be returning home alone, as her husband was afraid she would.

Her things were packed with as much haste as she could gather without appearing as though she was fleeing.

On her last night at court, the Queen beckoned her to come sit by her side.

"How is the baby?" she asked.

"Well, your grace. He kicks me all night," Margaret replied with a smile that told everyone she did not mind.

"You are fortunate. I wish to one day hold a baby of my own. Even to feel him kicking me would give me such comfort."

Margaret saw how wistful she looked. She believed, as many others did, that the Queen was infertile. This was her third marriage and she had never conceived, though her second marriage was to an old man. She had not realized how dearly Katherine wished for a child of her own.

"We all pray that Prince Edward will have a little brother to play with soon." She placed a hand over the Queen's and felt how cold they were. Was it fear?

"Regardless, I have all my step-children to look after." Katherine was smiling now. "You shall have to write to me about how the Lady Mary does. Make sure her household is running well."

"As you wish."

A heavy silence fell between them of things left unsaid. Neither dared say more. Margaret wished she could offer some sort of assistance but dared not. Besides, what influence did she have?

"I remain your loyal servant," she said, trying to find some happy middle ground. She did not call herself friend in case anyone overheard and thought she was supportive of the Queen's views. Nor would she willingly offer assistance to the opposition. She liked this Queen and, more than anything, was tired of seeing them come and go.

Katherine seemed to understand.

Margaret was happy to be packed off in a litter. She

sent off a letter to Scotland before she departed, in case Matthew was able to come home or write to her.

———

The roads were packed with stragglers and beggars. Margaret had a coin purse distributed among them. It was empty well before they left the gates of London. It was hard to ignore how the roads felt less safe. The monasteries used to feed the poor and provide them with shelter but none remained. Now desperate times had led to some taking matters into their own hands. With no work, many turned to thievery to survive.

Margaret drew the curtains of her litter and ordered her escort to draw in closer — she felt ill at ease.

When she arrived at Mary's house, workmen were setting up scaffolding to repair some windows and trim the vine growing along the house. Mary greeted her with a warm embrace.

"I am glad you were willing to travel in your condition," she said, taking on a decidedly motherly tone.

"Nothing I have not done before." Margaret waved off her concerns.

"Any news from your husband?" Mary asked as they walked inside. Margaret going much slower, as she had become stiff from sitting all day in the litter.

The servants would carry in the trunks and her maid would unpack her things. She wasn't sure how long she would stay, but she now saw herself heading for her home rather than going back to court.

A letter arrived from her husband — he was in York. Margaret was surprised by this but glad he was safe on English soil. The letter went on to say that he was riding with all haste for London — he would not stop to see her at Temple Newsham though he hoped to be with her soon.

What could have happened?

The letter did not say but she knew it was nothing good.

William notified her of her husband's arrival.

Breaking with all conventions or thoughts for her condition, she found herself running down to the courtyard — although at this point the most she could manage was a quick gait.

"Mathieu," she called out to him, almost disbelieving he was here. She knew she was gaping at him as if he were an apparition that appeared before her.

She let him pull her close and place a kiss that lingered longer than it should have, given their audience.

"You have returned?"

"I have," he released her, studying her as she studied him.

She saw his road weary face and, beneath the grime, the exhaustion that lay there.

"You shall not leave," she all but commanded. "I am

to go into confinement soon, and I should like to celebrate the New Year with you in our home with our son."

"It shall be as you wish," he promised her.

Margaret ordered a bath to be brought up for Matthew and fresh clothes laid out. She wished to have the ones he currently wore to be burned away, but she thought she would be frugal and just send them to the laundry.

The days grew shorter as December approached. The golden autumn leaves fell, leaving the trees bare. Meanwhile, Margaret continued growing plumper and plumper.

She was in confinement with her ladies, tapestries covering the walls and windows to keep all evil spirits out. Matthew visited her daily and they spoke through the barrier — the priest also came to pray with her.

With her previous pregnancy she had been kept bored out of her mind, but this time she was so tired she just slept most of the day and, when she could, she would stitch embroidery into little clothes made for the baby kicking around in her belly.

She eagerly awaited his arrival — the fear of child-birth far out of her mind.

So when her waters broke in the middle of the night she cheerfully called for the midwife to come. This birth was easier than the last, even more of a joy was the squalling bundle they handed to her. Her baby boy with his pink skin and blonde wispy hair looked like an angel.

They decided to name him Henry.

She wrote to the Lady Mary and the King of his arrival and awaited their replies and gifts.

Her little Henry was perfect. She could tell that he was a strong fighter — he would have a brilliant future. She was sure of it.

---

The King was ill.

There was no hiding it after he couldn't even make an appearance at the New Year's celebrations. The throne remained empty as the court made merry. His health had been failing for quite some time, but everyone seemed to know that this time was different. Now they tiptoed around court as if they all knew a secret, one that they dared not name: that soon there would be a new King.

Prince Edward was still so young — barely nine years old. There would have to be a long regency before he would reach his majority. That meant instability, possibly civil war.

Margaret was often at court with her son — a young precocious boy that ran around the Queen's rooms until he had caused enough damage that he was sent away with his nurse.

She was pregnant once more and she wondered how she would handle two unruly children. Henry was loud and demanding as Margaret would always complain, but she could never bring herself to say no to her precious son.

"I am sorry I seem to be lax with my duties as one of your chief ladies," Margaret said, patting her rounded belly. "I seem to be available only for a few months out of the year."

The Queen laughed. "Well, if you keep making such beautiful children, I shall forgive you."

Henry sat in her lap as she stroked his golden curls. He smiled up at her, even at such a young age he liked receiving compliments.

"Have you seen the King today?" Margaret asked.

The Queen nodded. "I sat with him, reading some papers but they seemed to bring him little joy. He needed some rest."

Ever since the inquiry into her lectures and religion, the Queen had tread a careful path — never straying from what her husband thought was acceptable. She had very nearly lost her head — a thought that seemed to haunt her every day.

Margaret, who had known her for a very long time, could see from the way she dressed carefully, to the way she spoke and ensured she was never alone, that she was being cautious to not give anyone cause to gossip.

It irked Margaret that she and her children were written out of the succession charter that her uncle had passed. She felt this was unfair, especially because the children of her aunt had not been. Why did her cousins have right to the English throne and she did not?

Matthew was not concerned with this — as a person with a claim to a throne himself he had learned not to put much stock in such things. If you did not have the backing of the people, it did not matter if you were the next in line for the throne — they would throw you down.

He was still irritated that he had, as of yet, failed to recuperate his lands in Scotland. He fretted over the financial security of his family. Her uncle saw him as a failure and blamed him for the failed campaign in Scotland. Now the young Queen Mary was in France, betrothed to the future King. This alliance was a danger to England, and instead of blaming himself for not sending a large enough army and enough supplies, he blamed his generals.

The situation had remained tense for many months. Margaret was too scared to ask her uncle for a grant of money to repair the stables at Temple Newsham.

Lady Anne Stanhope was peacocking around court. As the wife of the prince's uncle — a man who was sure to be influential in the new court — people had begun deferring to her. She was throwing her weight around too.

It irritated Queen Katherine to no end, but she could not say anything explicitly to her.

For Margaret this was even more personal. All the rewards were being lavished on Edward Seymour — the King favored Lady Anne as well. They were also part of the reformers at court whereas, she was still strongly identified with the old religion.

She felt sidelined but at the same time it did not seem to bother Katherine and her cousin, the Lady Mary, who was still a staunch Catholic though she only privately had mass said and communicated with the Spanish Emperor through the ambassador.

The Lady Mary still remained unmarried after all of these years. A French match had been proposed but her father had decided against it after they had taken in the Queen of Scots.

Margaret wondered what was to become of her cousin who was once a princess and the sole heiress to the crown of England.

---

"How could they not issue us with black cloth from the royal wardrobe?" Margaret fumed.

"Darling, I warned you this may happen," Matthew said with a shrug. He moved out of the way as a manservant carried a trunk out of the room.

"I am the cousin of the King, beloved niece to the old King — God rest his soul," she continued her tirade. "I should..."

"It does not matter."

Margaret was taken aback by his frankness.

"We shall pay for it out of our own coffers — I will not let you be upstaged by the ladies at court or look dowdy, if that is what concerns you."

She wasn't reassured. "We need to cement our position. We are a part of the royal family."

"We are not part of the new privy council. I was not named and Edward Seymour has named himself Lord

Protector. It is the Seymours and their affinity that are in the ascendency."

"Why couldn't you have been named?" Margaret continued to rail against their rotten luck.

"It does not matter. Those around the King at the time of his death took matters into their own hands. He wanted a regency council to rule until Edward came of age, but it seems that Seymour will rule the country. We missed our chance."

"Several chances." She pinched the bridge of her nose. "Well they better pay our allowance as before."

Matthew turned more serious now. "We shall have to be careful. I managed to squirrel away some savings, but we shall have to hope they honor our agreement with your uncle. They won't let us fall into poverty. We have some rents from the lands your uncle gave us."

"They are barely enough to cover our basic expenses."

"Then we shall tighten our belts."

He laughed, seeing her grimace. "We shall have to make due."

There was no point arguing further. She hoped that she would be able to ingratiate herself with the new King — she also hoped that her son would be able to join his playmates. Of course he was too young now, but he was already such a talented boy.

The family was on its way as fast as they could to London to attend the funeral — and then they would stay until the coronation.

It was no longer the now dowager Queen Katherine that ruled the roost. As predicted, Lady Anne was walking around court as if she was in charge. Margaret felt this was highly irregular — out of spite, she avoided her and stayed mostly with Katherine.

"I plan to retire to my manor at Chelsea," Katherine told her.

"Does the King not want you here? He carries such affection for you."

"I am afraid he is being kept awfully busy. Too busy for his stepmother. Though he finds time to send me notes," she admitted.

"I cannot believe that."

"Oh it is not so hard to imagine," Katherine said. "I am of no use now. Though everyone wonders if I could be with child. I think they would prefer if I packed myself away from their sight. It's a new world — a new regime."

"The Seymours cannot rule over everything."

"You will find that they can." Katherine shrugged. "I have little power now. I shall go try to carve a bit of happiness for myself."

"At Chelsea?" Margaret was incredulous.

"At Chelsea," Katherine confirmed. She had a far off look on her face. Perhaps, she was indeed happy to rest.

# CHAPTER 4

## 1547-1548

MARGARET FORMALLY PRESENTED her son to the young King. Her son performed his little bow well for one so young. She was taken aback by Edward's cool behavior.

"It pleases us to welcome my dear cousin Margaret." Already he was looking past her as though bored.

"Thank you, your grace." Margaret found her mouth dry. "I was hoping you would like to take Lord Darnley into your household to be raised with your grace."

Before the King could speak, Somerset materialized by his side.

"Unfortunately, there are no openings in the King's household. It is highly irregular to trouble the King with such matters," he said, as though he were scolding Margaret.

She bit her tongue lest she say something offensive.

"I shall not trouble your grace any longer." She placed a hand on her child's shoulders and ushered him out of the chamber, careful not to make eye contact with Somerset.

---

Her husband was in his private study at Temple Newsham, poring over documents. A man was standing by the window, waiting patiently. Margaret did not recognize him; she wondered if Matthew was hiring someone new.

"May I speak to you?" she asked him, avoiding the stranger's gaze. "Alone, of course."

Matthew sighed but nodded. "Roger, you will wait outside."

"Of course, milord."

Margaret thought she heard the hint of Scottish in his accent.

She walked around to stand beside Matthew, looking at his papers. Notes and letters — many seemed nonsensical.

"Who are all these from?" She picked one up, scanning it.

"First, tell me what you wanted to say."

"I suppose you know," she said, putting the paper down. "I feel completely ostracized by Somerset. He has no right to act so high and mighty. I have royal blood."

"He is in charge now. Or at least for the time being, you have to find a way to work with him. Make your peace with the fact we no longer have the influence we once did."

"And what are you doing? How is this helping ensure a brilliant future for our son?"

"Margaret, I don't appreciate it when you talk to me like I'm some idiot page boy that dropped the ink pot." He motioned for her to sit.

"Since you will probably see it in our ledgers, I might as well tell you now that I have hired several men to gather information for me. So you see I am about to make myself useful to Somerset, and thus, I hope to gain his favor."

Margaret scowled. "You are paying for spies?"

"I can see you are displeased by the notion, but since brute force did not work at bringing the Scottish lords to heel, perhaps cunning will do the trick."

"Will this help get our lands back?"

"Will you make peace with your father?"

She rolled her eyes. "You know I am right. He should have supported me. Us! He abandoned you and the English King when he had promised to be loyal. He does not even name me his heir."

"Things are complicated. Things are different now. We will adjust."

"How can you be so... accepting of this?"

"Maggie, my life has been nothing but adapting. I learned early on that the world does not bend to my will. I was born in Scotland, raised in France. I now live in England married to an English woman. I have lost my birthright and now I shall fight for its return probably to my very last breath for our family and my son." He paused, taking a breath to calm himself. "You shall have to learn to adapt — you have been raised by a doting uncle who has allowed you certain liberties. Now that he is gone you must adjust."

"He was hardly doting." Margaret was too proud to concede he was right, and he was too loving to press the matter further.

"I will hopefully manage to ingratiate myself with the new regime. Our fortunes shall improve. Don't worry yourself so much in your condition. Go play with Henry, it always lifts your spirits."

"I shall but not because you told me to." She gave him a quick peck and left him to his work.

Perhaps he would succeed and become influential enough to ask for Darnley to be brought up at court with Edward. It was only right that cousins were raised together.

---

Their fall from grace seemed to bring more trouble to their doorstep than just an insecure income. After Mass on Sunday, in their private chapel, the priest asked if he might have a private word with them.

"Is something the matter?" Matthew was sitting behind his desk looking serious.

Margaret could see the stacks of unread missives piled on the bookshelf behind him. He had a lot of work to do.

"Well, my lord. It is just that I was speaking to Father Paul and he mentioned that some of the congregation have been making trouble." Father Paul gave sermons to their servants and the locals around the community at the church nearby. A church Margaret paid quarterly sums to ensure there was proper funds to run such a godly place — it was also where her first son was buried.

"Some were heard speaking out against the mass — they said this was 'popeish' heresy," he continued.

Margaret gasped. "We have never had trouble before."

Matthew placed a hand to motion her to be silent.

"You have names of these people and the crimes they have been accused of committing ready I assume?"

"Yes, I do milord."

"Good. I shall send them along to London. As for any members of my household that are acting against the laws of the church, I shall have them sent from here to prison if it is the wish of the King and his council."

"Heretics should be burned. If Lutherans have infiltrated our community they must be made an example of." A cold look had come over the priest.

"If that is the will of the King but it is not within our power to lay such serious punishments. I would have the Archbishop rule on what is to be done." With that, Matthew dismissed the priest who was clearly disappointed by his lack of zeal.

Margaret, who had watched this exchange, couldn't help but question her husband.

"Maggie, the King is a Protestant. Who knows what is allowed any more? He sets the rules."

"The bible does. My uncle sinned when he separated

the church from Rome."

"You may believe that, but keep it to yourself. Be careful — I don't want us to go against the new regime or be accused of some sort of conspiracy."

Regardless of what Matthew wanted she purged the household of undesirables trying to stir up trouble and gossiping about her Catholicism.

How dare they even think to question their lord and lady? Upsetting the natural order of things was just more evidence of how wrong this Protestant hearsay was.

Her husband found himself called back to court periodically. Somerset had work for him, but it was clear that he wasn't trusted. Though he conformed to the Protestant faith, many knew of his true leanings especially because his wife had not yet ceased to hear mass.

Finally, he was sent to Scotland to fight alongside the English, leaving Margaret to bear the separation alone. If it wasn't for her son she would have been heartbroken by the constant loneliness.

Her uncle's old plan of uniting the Kingdoms through the marriage of Edward and the Queen of Scots was in full swing once again. Mary Queen of Scots was the most eligible match in the Christian world.

Her dowry was a whole Kingdom.

It mattered a bit more to the English, who were worried that whoever she married would basically gain a backdoor to England. Their north would be utterly exposed if the French were to invade through Scotland.

So it was important to see the little Queen barely out of her cradle tied in marriage to an Englishman who would keep the Scots loyal.

PART TWO



*For whereas I love faithfully, I know he will*
*Not slack his love, nor never change his fantasy*

*- Margaret Douglas, Countess of Lennox*

# CHAPTER 5

## 1552

ON A CRISP AUTUMN DAY, Margaret received a letter from Scotland, and surprisingly it was not from her husband but her father. She tore the seal off the letter without much preamble. She wondered what he was accusing her of now.

Instead she found words of apology and the sad news of the death of her half-brother.

The sorrow of losing a child was well known to her. Already the workers had begun work on the chiseled effigy for her children. How many young souls would be buried there? She treasured Henry even more now. He was a tall seven-year-old who had retained his beautiful golden hair. She still oversaw his schedule every day and ensured he only rode the safest horses, though his tutor said he had a natural gift with horses.

Her thoughts turned from her golden son to her father in cold bleary Scotland.

He was all alone now. Except for her.

She was filled with the desire to see her father and embrace him. It had been so many years since she had last laid eyes on him. He must have grown old during this time. She bit her lip. Would it be wrong to wish to see him?

They had fought but they were also family and that list was growing ever shorter with the passing years.

She did not have to pray on it long.

But she also could not just pack her things and cross the border. She would have to write to the King's council and the King himself for permission to travel. For good measure, she also informed her husband of her decision to join him in Scotland.

In the meantime, she would move the household from Temple Newsham to Stephney Palace to be closer to the border.

On her way, she decided to take a detour to visit Lady Mary. It had been ages since she had seen her.

Ever since Mary had begun her passive war against the King's council by refusing to stop hearing mass, she had become a hero to many of the old faith, herself included. She wished she was stronger and had more resolve but she feared the axe. Mary had the protection of her uncle the Emperor Charles — but no one would speak out on Margaret's behalf. Or at least no one important.

Mary was surprised but pleased to see her. Young Henry ran around her rooms, fetching things for her, determined to act as her page boy for the duration of his visit.

"I see he is already devoted to you." Margaret laughed as he pressed a flower into Mary's warm hands.

"I am honored," she said, as a smile spread across her face. She seemed disused to smiling.

These last few years must have been hard on her. They had been hard on her as well, Margaret noted, though perhaps she had aged better. They had been young cousins, and now they would become old ladies together. She shook her head of the image of them grey and wrinkled, sitting before a fire as they were now.

There was no point worrying about the inevitable. If they could even last that long.

"They arrested my chaplain," Mary said, nonchalant as ever. "I fear they shall try to arrest all those they fear of being followers of the true faith."

"Their tolerance grows thinner with each passing year." Margaret bit her lip to stop herself from asking her cousin if she would desist in her ways. She did not wish to see her imprisoned.

"The King will come into his majority soon."

Mary laughed. It was a harsh barking sound. "According to Lord Dudley, he has already reached his majority." She shook her head. "No, even when he does, there is no hope. God forgive me but it would take a miracle for my brother to shake off the lies he has been taught and fed since he was a babe."

"This is something we pray for, though I dare not do so openly," Margaret said, her voice soft as though she was pleading forgiveness.

"I know you are loyal," Mary reassured her. "You

have remained my most steadfast friend during these troubled times."

"There are many others who feel the same way." Margaret was not exaggerating. How many secret messages had found their way into her hands? She burned letters every day, not daring to incriminate herself or her family.

"And tell me of your father. Are you excited to be going back to Scotland?" Mary changed the subject smoothly as a chambermaid came in with fresh linen for the bed.

"We have exchanged a few letters. Truthfully, I remember nothing about Scotland. As you know, I was even born on this side of the Northern border. I barely remember my own mother."

"It is strange how the passage of time changes a person. Even makes them forget," Mary said.

Margaret wondered if Mary would ever forget her own mother. It felt as though she was still fighting a war for her freedom. The battle that began when she was a teenager continued raging on even though she was now a middle-aged woman. She snapped herself out of reminiscing and feeling sorry for herself.

"We were blessed with fathers that were difficult to please. But we must press on. I hope that now we can make amends and that he shall support my husband's claim to his lands," Margaret said, not adding that she hoped for more for herself as well.

If she could be named his heir, then she would have even greater wealth. If he could finally acknowledge her properly, perhaps they could enjoy a few happy years together. She never knew the love of a parent, and now, having her own children made her dearly wish for that love she gave to them.

She spent a few more days in Mary's company, spending time with her cousin as they talked of the old days before it was finally time to pack up once more and leave. Her steward made sure everyone was ready to depart, while her treasurer worried over the costs that this delay to their journey had caused.

"There will be nothing for it milady," he said. "If we are not careful we may fall into debt this year."

Margaret laughed at his fears. "Do not worry so much. I shall find ways to fill our coffers. I can even write to the King my nephew," she reminded him gently.

He looked skeptical; after all, what did a woman like her know? He did not know of her great expectations.

---

Scotland was indeed wild but it was a beautiful wilderness. The sprawling emerald green grass over the hills and the fresh crisp air were a balm for the soul. They lifted her spirits and she did not even fear as her large retinue traveled through forests where the undergrowth had grown so thick you could barely see.

Her father's men had met her at the border and were escorting her to what should have been her home. What might still be...

She was surprised to find that the castles and cities in

Scotland were not much different from England. There were less houses of leisure — most castles and palaces were heavily defended by moats and walls. These were not like Hampton Court Palace built for show and entertainment but for defense and attack.

Still the people were civilized and they seemed to pay her every respect.

Her father greeted her with a large banquet. Two large boars were roasting on a spit in his hall, as carvers doled out portions to each lord and lady in attendance. Most were his tenants or those of his clan — her distant cousins that she had never met.

Much was made of young Darnley, who loved being put on display and, like a peacock, strutted proudly by his grandfather's side.

Despite their warm welcome, Margaret was feeling apprehensive now.

She had never been anything but brave on paper. Often, she remembered how brazen she had been in her letters to him. But now in person, she found her tongue had been silenced. She was no longer comfortable enough to broach the subject of her inheritance and it was tearing her up.

At night, she tossed and turned, and was suddenly homesick for her own rooms at Temple Newsham.

It took several days but she finally had to ask.

"My lord father, I assume you have invited me here because you wish to alter your will. I believe that as your only legitimate living heir, I am entitled to this."

He surprised her by laughing. She watched his grey beard twitch with mirth.

"Yes, indeed you are my last legitimate heir, though your mother claimed otherwise when she divorced me."

"I am here to try to make amends."

"You were raised in England, you need to understand this. You were even born there." He looked apologetic. "Your husband does not have much support among the nobles. If you were to inherit my land and titles, you would not be allowed to keep it long."

"But..."

He continued, interrupting her.

"There is nothing I can do about that. Perhaps, if things change while I am still alive, I can make this happen for you." He shook his head. "But truthfully, your husband cannot regain his own lands, so he shall never be able to hold on to mine. Additionally, how would it look if you inherited mine and your husband got his. It would look as though the pair of you would be readying to claim Scotland for yourselves. The lords would never allow it."

"That is not what we would be doing." She did not say that they had no interest in the Scottish crown. "I would return to live in England."

"Which is a problem as well. How are you to rule over my lands from England?" he asked her plainly.

"There are ways..." She imagined she would hire a loyal man to oversee things here.

"It would be seen as the first step in the English invasion. Or rather in another English invasion. There is little love for the English at this time. I took a great risk even asking you here. I hope you can see that. If it is money you are after — do not fear, I have provided for you in my will, but I can do nothing more."

She watched him study her face.

"I can see you have the Douglas stubbornness in you," he said approvingly. "Perhaps you are wondering if this journey was in vain, but I am an old man now and I wished to see my daughter and grandson before I departed this world. I have never been a father to you but now at least I can try to make amends by spending the last few months I have left with you."

She looked down ashamed at her own greed. She would have to confess this sin to the priest.

"I am glad I have come. I always wished to know my father better and now God has graced me this chance."

He patted her arm. "I shall make sure you are never bored nor lonely."

---

It was her father that brought her the news. Pale faced and mournful as though he wished this task had not come upon him.

"What is it?" Margaret all but yanked the letter out of his hands. It was the seal of the privy council.

"Terrible news, I am afraid." He looked even more grave. "The English King Edward is dead and they have placed your cousin Jane Grey on the throne."

It took a moment for Margaret to process what he had said.

"How can that be? That goes against the line of succession. Princess Mary was next."

He shook his head. "I fear that the timing of your being allowed to come to Scotland was all too convenient. Write immediately to your husband."

"I still don't understand. What has happened to Princess Mary?" Margaret imagined her imprisoned in the Tower.

"The latest report says that she has fled north, but she must bend to the will of the privy council or else pray that her Spanish relatives come to her aid."

Margaret bit her lip. "This is impossible. I cannot believe this. And my poor cousin! What was it that killed him?"

"They say it was an illness — he was never a strong boy," her father replied.

She wondered what else? Lady Jane Grey had been recently married to Dudley's son — had this mysterious illness really been the work of God, or did man's hand have some part to play? She would pray for the soul of her poor cousin.

"Any news from my husband?"

"None yet, but I will send for you the minute I hear anything."

"Thank you," she said, placing a hand on her head as though to still her thoughts. "I must go somewhere and think."

He handed her the letter. "Read this if you can decipher some hidden meaning from it. I am not as attuned to English politics as I once was."

She retreated to her rooms, reading by candlelight the missive from England.

Before she did anything else she wrote to Princess Mary addressing her as such. Not caring who would read.

*"Dear Princess Mary,*

*Please write to me of your news and how I am to serve you?*

*I have heard you have been unjustly deprived of your crown, and I wish to know what I could do to help you. I fear I am trapped in Scotland and fear that if I cross the border before I know how things are in England that I may be placed under arrest.*

*Let me know of anything I can do for you.*

*Yours,*

*Margaret, Countess of Lennox.*

She then wrote to her husband, asking for further instruction. Would there be an all out civil war? She imagined that several people had been unhappy under Edward's regime. He had been a puppet to greater men; now would they tolerate a deviation from the law?

Margaret would place a bet that this would not end well. The council was not all powerful. They had the English people to answer to, and the people loved their Princess Mary. In the past they had even risen up against the King to have her mother reinstated at his side and her back in line for the throne.

They waited for news. She could not do anything from Scotland, and she dared not return to England.

In the end, she had nothing to fear. Her husband wrote to her that Dudley failed to capture Mary, and she had rallied the people to her cause. Dudley's army had refused to fight for him, and they had failed to engage Mary's army. So his army fled while hers had marched peacefully to London as though on parade rather than on campaign.

Queen Jane had barely ruled for over a week before she was overthrown. Now she awaited her fate in the Tower.

Margaret couldn't really recall Jane Grey — her cousin had been younger than even the Lady Elizabeth and hardly worth her notice.

Now that she knew of how matters stood in England, she did not even wait for the royal summons. She began packing up to leave.

Her fortunes had shifted once more.

# CHAPTER 6

## 1553-1554

THE LEAVES WERE TURNING red and golden hues as Queen Mary was crowned. There was much rejoicing in the city of London.

A huge dais was erected upon which awaited Mary's throne. Margaret watched in awe as her cousin ascended the steps, the swish of the luxurious purple velvet gown she wore and the sparkle of the coronet caught her eye.

The magnitude of this occasion was not lost on Margaret. England now had a Queen.

The first Queen who would rule in her own right.

Margaret must have been lost in her thoughts because she suddenly found the whole congregation shouting "God Save Queen Mary."

She joined in with her own exuberant cries.

The Queen was generous to them. A bounty beyond her imagining.

They had some of the best rooms at Whitehall Palace and precedence over every other lady except the Lady

Elizabeth who had emerged as her sister's most ardent supporter.

Margaret couldn't help but sneer at the redheaded chit who moved around court in her dark dresses, a contrast to the richly dressed women. She acted pious but in truth she was setting herself apart from the Catholics — reminding the worried Protestants there was another heir, one more amenable to their cause.

Matthew did not entertain her conspiracy theories by listening to her. He told her that he would hear none of it and that for once they were to be happy.

"The Queen is offering her full support in helping to regain my Scottish lands — she has already written to Mary of Guise on my behalf. She has granted us a considerable annuity and we are clearly favored." He kissed her forehead. "I shall not hear of any complaints from you."

"They are not complaints," Margaret protested. She removed her gable hood scratching at her scalp. "My head hurts."

He came up behind her and massaged her neck. She sighed happily at his ministrations.

"Maybe once it stops hurting, you shall see how much you have to be thankful for," he said.

"Please, don't get me wrong, I am on my knees every night thanking my lucky stars."

He laughed. "Do you thank them for me as well?" He leaned forward placing a kiss at the nape of her neck.

She blushed red. "Honestly, Mathieu, you would think we were newly married. Many men would have bored with their wives by now and moved on to a mistress or two."

"Is that what you want me to do?" His whisper in her ear sent a shiver coursing through her.

She turned around, a grin on her face. "Of course not. But we must go down to dinner."

"Must we? I am sure we can be a bit late."

Now it was her turn to laugh, and in a good mood, let him pull her to their bed. Perhaps she would conceive a healthy child this time around. Darnley needed a sibling.

---

A new Spanish Ambassador arrived with all due haste and Mary planned a great banquet. She was resolute that England would ally itself with the Spanish, even though her courtiers grumbled. The Spanish had never been trustworthy, and the courtiers feared that Queen Mary would be easily influenced by her relations.

Before the occasion, Mary had named Lennox as her Master of Hawks. His duties came with an annual fee as well that pleased Margaret. She had discovered she was with child again, and the added expense to the household would be significant.

Over twenty tapestries had been sent to her to decorate her rooms with and a beautiful gown of gold thread to match the Queen's own. Margaret could not thank her enough.

"You shall wear it at the banquet," Mary commanded with a smile. Her face went sour when she spotted her sister sewing by the fire in her dark velvet gown. "And Lady Elizabeth you shall be sure to dress in one of the many fine gowns I have gifted you as well."

Margaret saw Elizabeth shoot a glance at Lady Kat Ashley, but she turned a smiling face to her sister.

"I fear that they do not become me as they do you. I do not wish to sparkle and shine."

"It is my express wish that you do so." Mary's voice was now tense.

"Of course, your majesty."

Margaret knew that she would find a way to disobey her sister. Elizabeth seemed to be chafing under Mary's rule. Even though Mary had been nothing but cordial to her. She also remembered how Elizabeth had been perfectly fine to wear brightly colored gowns of red and green. She loved finery just as much as Mary had. This latest conversion was more likely an exercise in public relations rather than her true preference.

"Perhaps your sister would wish to join a nunnery," Margaret said to Mary under her breath. "For she seems so utterly devoted to living in silence and humility."

She was rewarded with Mary's laughter.

"I doubt it. That gown she is wearing costs more than my own. It seems plain but the cloth is the finest to be had."

"Of course, and those pearls in her French hood are huge."

"It has not escaped my notice. She might give the appearance of plainness, but she is just as extravagant as the rest of us." Mary sighed. "I wish I could force her to come to mass. All my attempts thus far have failed."

"She was raised with heretics and practiced the Protestant faith most openly."

"My advisors say I cannot go around prosecuting everyone who followed my father's changes and then my brother's. But I have written to the Pope and he assures me that he shall welcome the English back into the fold when it is time."

"That is the most wonderful news," Margaret exclaimed. She was thinking of the chantry she could reopen to say prayers for the souls of her departed children. It filled her with such happiness.

"And have you decided what to do with Jane Grey?" Margaret asked, remembering suddenly the girl locked away in the Tower.

"Not yet. I wish to set her free. She was nothing more than a pawn. She does not deserve to suffer because of the crimes of other men. My council remain resolute that I keep her imprisoned."

"What harm can she do now? The people have clearly chosen."

"She would be the center of rebellion or at least that is what they say. The Protestants looks to her."

"Is Elizabeth not just as much of a risk?" Margaret asked this in a whisper.

"Yes," Mary said without hesitation. "But she has done nothing that I could send her to the Tower for. She belongs there, not that sweet girl Jane. Elizabeth is cunning and careful, but if she steps one toe out of line, I shall know how to deal with her. I would not hesitate. She is infuriating."

Margaret nodded. She looked at the redhead, sitting pretty as a picture.

She looked young and vivacious, whereas Mary had begun to look worn. The constant battles with her councils over what should be done and what direction to take the country in was sapping her strength.

"They are insisting I begin to look for a husband," Mary said with an air of disgust. "I am barely a month on the throne and already they seek out a King."

"Who would you marry?"

Mary looked away as though she had a wish already. "They have suggested a few names, but I shall write to my cousin the Emperor and seek his advice. I do not trust these turncoats to have my best interests at heart." She laughed when she saw her face.

"Oh yes, most are turncoats. They were quick to declare loyalty for me when I had won, but they had been supporting Dudley before. I will never forget this. But I need them. Perhaps, over time, I shall inspire true love and loyalty in them, but I will not hold my breath." She sighed.

"I am so grateful to have you by my side."

Margaret did not know what to say. How troublesome the crown seemed to be, but all the same, she could not help but wish she had it in her grasp as well.

The banquet was the grandest of Queen Mary's reign. Musicians never ceased playing for the duration of the day, nor did the stream of entertainment ever seem to end.

The Spanish Ambassador was celebrated with all the pomp and ceremony a visiting monarch might expect to receive. From his furtive glances, Margaret suspected he was feeling awkward about the importance he was given. After all, the Spanish had not been supportive of Mary's campaign to capture her throne.

Mary seemed to have forgotten this completely, for she was all smiles and promised to give him a private audience the following day. Margaret watched this from her side. She was dressed in the gold gown from the Queen, and Mary seemed keen on pressing her forward.

"May I introduce my dearest cousin Margaret, Countess of Lennox," Queen Mary said, leading him over to her.

"It is a pleasure to meet you, Countess. You are radiant." He placed a kiss on her outstretched hand.

With the candlelight flickering all about her, she was sure the gold thread of her gown was indeed sparkling. She noted with a bit of mirth that the ambassador was short and had a dark sort of appearance that reminded her of a moor. Perhaps he was a converso — newly converted to the Catholic faith.

At this moment, Darnley chose to approach his mother, wishing for her attention. He tugged on her sleeve in a most childish manner.

"Darling, your mama is busy right now. Please greet the Spanish Ambassador." She pressed him forward.

As if he was an actor in a play, he turned very serious as he looked up at the stranger, knowing well enough that the word ambassador meant he was a very important man. Margaret hid a smile as he doffed his cap and bowed from the waist, his back straight.

"How do you do, monsieur?" He spoke a little French.

As he did so, Margaret scanned him for any dirt or grime but found him perfectly tidy and she breathed a sigh of relief. He was dressed in a handsome cream suit, threaded with gold to match her own dress. A rich costume fine for any prince.

The Ambassador seemed to note this as well.

"Do you speak anything else besides French, Lord Darnley?" he inquired with mock seriousness.

"I am learning Latin and a bit of Greek, though my tutor says I do not have the patience for it." He replied with the brutal honesty of a young child.

"Why, you must apply yourself more then and prove him wrong."

"I shall do so," he promised and Margaret placed two hands on his shoulders to lead him away. She gave Mary a little curtsey and excused herself.

When they were out of earshot, Margaret asked him where his nurse was.

"I don't know." He shrugged.

"Did you escape from her, you naughty boy?"

He grinned up at her.

"Darnley, you must not do that. Try to remember to act dignified."

She could tell the word dignified meant nothing to him, nor did her scolding seem to affect him. She sighed. Sometimes she worried she was too indulgent of a mother. Scanning the crowd, she spotted the nurse looking anxiously around for her charge among the guests.

Margaret sent Darnley to go to her.

"Behave yourself or I shall not bring you again," she said, though it was an empty threat.

Margaret kept her eyes fixed on him as he bounded off. She smiled at his blonde curls escaping his hat and bouncing as he walked. He was such a sweet little thing.

When she returned to Mary's side, she found that the two of them had been watching her.

"You are a very indulgent mother, Countess."

"I am guilty of that," she replied with a laugh.

"My cousin is the gentlest of women and very loyal," Queen Mary heaped on the praise.

Margaret looked between the two of them.

"Have you been discussing something in regards to me?" she finally asked.

"Her Majesty was informing me of your many adventures together."

Margaret knew this wasn't quite the truth. Perhaps, when the chance presented itself, she would ask Mary herself when they were alone together.

The night pressed on. Margaret took the chance to dance with her husband several times. Their stars had finally risen and who knew how far they would be able to go yet?

---

"Do you think such a thing would succeed?" Matthew was incredulous.

They were at Temple Newsham waiting for Margaret to be churched following the birth of a baby girl they had christened Matilda. She was a sweet babe with Margaret's eyes but Matthew's coloring.

"Why should it not?" Margaret threw back at him. "The Queen spoke to me herself, she is conferring with Renard as we now speak. Lady Elizabeth is still refusing to attend mass and Mary has her doubts."

"Doubts about what?"

"Her validity," Margaret said, as if this should be obvious.

He frowned. "Yours would be in question just as much. Your parents divorced."

"The Pope has declared their marriage was valid and that I am legitimate. The Lady Elizabeth may only be the bastard of Queen Anne and that poet. He had red hair as well you know."

"The King would not have been cuckolded like that. She is the very image of him."

Margaret shrugged. "Who's to say? Besides, her mother lost her head for being a harlot."

"That is very crass of you. How many secret

marriages and betrothals did you enter into before we were married?"

Now it was Margaret who felt her temper rising.

"Are you seriously bringing that up again?"

"My sweet Maggie, you know I do not care. We love each other. What has happened in the past is in the past. But do you think that others would not bring it up just as quickly as you question Lady Elizabeth's parentage? They could also use the same logic to question the validity of our marriage and the legitimacy of our children."

She gasped. "None would dare!"

"Not now." He held her hands, smoothing them with caresses. "We are the favorites now. Given our places and titles, but if we were to be elevated above the norm, we would have a line of people ready to drag us down." He paused. "There is no point arguing over this. There is no chance anything will happen. We do not have enough support and the English Parliament will never stand for it. Besides, the Queen may choose to marry and if God wishes it may grant her an heir of her body to inherit the crown so all this speculation will have been for nothing."

"Do you not wish to wear a crown?" she whispered.

"I am not so ambitious." He shook his head. "It is not for lack of wanting power and riches, but the dangers are too great. I am not so blinded that I cannot see we would never succeed."

"Then I am a foolish woman."

"You are a dreamer." He released his hold on her.

Of course, her sliver of hope all came to nothing. The

Spanish Ambassador had spoken against elevating Margaret to be Mary's official heir and the lord privy seal did the same.

Queen Mary chafed under the knowledge she may be forced to name Elizabeth her heir. So her mind turned more favorably to the idea of marriage and producing a child of her own. Mary told her all of this in private as Margaret plaited her hair before bed.

"I shall speak to my privy council. If there is a candidate that God smiles upon, I shall do his bidding and marry for the good of the realm."

"You must do as your conscience bids you. Marriage has been a most happy estate for me." Margaret tried to keep the disappointment from her voice, but it strained her to do so.

Mary regarded her from the looking glass.

"I fear it had not been near the end for my mother. I fear the power a husband has over his wife."

Margaret knew there was little she could say in that regard.

"Then the choosing of a husband must be done with diligent care."

"You are right. I shall confer with the council, but I shall listen to what my heart tells me to do as well."

Margaret nodded. If it was not for her great age, Mary would have seemed as though she were a girl ready to fall in love.

Jane Dormer popped her head into the rooms and asked if she was ready for bed or if she wished for some entertainment.

"Not tonight, Jane. I think I shall pray at my prie-dieu before I go to bed."

Jane nodded.

She slept in the room with her mistress. Queen Mary was hardly left alone. There was always someone there. Someone to vouch for her virtue and safety.

———

"I hope you shall oblige me, Countess, and speak to her majesty about the benefits of Prince Philip as a prospective groom," the Spanish Ambassador said, with cheer in his voice as he pulled her aside from the other ladies of the Queen's retinue.

"I do not know enough of these matters to judge. I am sure the council will decide."

He shook his head. "They do not look favorably on a Spanish marriage, I am afraid."

"Then I should not dare to disagree with them," Margaret said, thinking of how the council also disagreed about naming her Mary's successor. The Spanish Ambassador had done nothing to disagree with them then.

But now she saw he was handing her some leverage with which she might use to further her own ends.

"I shall think about it," was all she said and promised.

Matthew had told her to leave this matter alone, but the thought of a crown had more than enticed her. She found herself unable to sleep at night, thinking of the rightness of her claim to the throne. She was English-born. She was legitimate. She was the niece of the King.

ANNE R BAILEY

She had produced a male heir. These were all very good reasons. Of course, what was missing was some serious political backing pushing this whole affair forward.

Indeed, upon deciding that she was the best candidate to be Mary's successor, she had begun looking down upon Lady Frances Grey, whose daughters still had a solid claim, despite Jane Grey being locked in the Tower and the Lady Elizabeth who she could barely treat with any sort of deference.

They had never been great friends, so if Elizabeth noticed she made no indication. Perhaps this irked her just as much. For she found that Elizabeth should not be ignoring her but rather trying to seek her favor.

So when Lady Elizabeth fainted from pain after being forced to attend chapel and had to be carried off by her attendants, Margaret scoffed at her and made sure to tell Queen Mary that she had seen her moments before mass had begun and she had been happy and laughing with some handsome man.

This was a fib but one that was just as likely to be true as to not be. Queen Mary seemed inclined to believe it as well.

In due course, the Ambassador produced a portrait of Prince Philip for Queen Mary to look over.

The portrait was hung in a private gallery. Margaret would have laughed at the importance given to this singular portrait, but she remembered how King Henry had treated the portrait of Anne of Cleves. Would Queen Mary remember how dissatisfied her father had been with the reality?

She would never dare broach the subject.

The man in the painting was young and handsome. He seemed to be well proportioned and had an expression that made him seem as though he was always ready to smile.

As she was standing to her left, Margaret heard Mary's intake of breath when it was revealed. The Queen took a step closer, then stepped back again fearing she had divulged some special interest.

"He is a handsome young man." The Spanish Ambassador had not missed the little movement.

"Perhaps he is too young." Queen Mary seemed to be backtracking.

Margaret could have laughed. It was as if they were bartering over horses at market day. One side extolled the virtues of the horse in question while the other side balked at the price and fretted over every little defect.

"He has been married before and is a man with many life experiences, so he is older beyond his years," Renard explained smoothly. He went on to list those many life experiences.

Margaret noted coyly how he seemed to have forgotten about Prince Philip's debts and the lovers that he left behind as he campaigned for his father around Europe. Was nothing to be said about that?

"He seems very serious," Margaret chimed in. Not

that the portrait could say as much. She would attribute it to the choice of dress.

"He is indeed. He takes his religion seriously as well. He sees it as his duty to defend Christendom and serve God." The Ambassador followed suit.

Mary nodded at this. She herself attributed her ascending the throne to God's divine will.

They went back and forth a bit longer before the interview ended. Mary asking more and more personal questions rather than worrying about statecraft. Her councilors could iron out the details of a treaty between England and Spain she wished to know about the man.

It was clear to Margaret and to everyone else that had been present that Queen Mary was very much inclined to accepting Prince Philip as her consort. This raised outrage among many, but as nothing official had been declared, people were content to murmur disapprovingly about the match. They envisioned being dragged into expensive wars, being absorbed by the Spanish Empire.

Meanwhile, Mary was in a joyous mood — oblivious to all for now.

The thought of her future happiness made her generous to those in the Tower. Several prisoners were released. Edward Courtney emerged from his dungeon cell a dazed but enamored subject of the Queen.

He was in fact her second cousin, with a claim to the English throne. As a child he had been imprisoned for the blood he carried and the aspirations of his father. Margaret saw him as a puppy dog, following at Queen Mary's heels wherever she went. Everything from the clothes on his back, to the jewel in his cap was all thanks to her.

But he was more than grateful, he claimed he was in love.

He wrote her pretty poems and put some of the words to music, but the Queen seemed oblivious to his attentions or she thought he would not take it any further than courtly love. Her mind was in far off Spain.

She wrote often to her cousin the Emperor while the privy council buckled down and sent a serious delegation to test the waters and see what a marriage with Spain might entail.

The Spanish Ambassador was often in the Queen's company and, thus, in her own. Margaret had a private understanding with him now that she would support his master's ambitions to see his son marry the Queen of England and in return he would encourage the Queen to write to Mary of Guise to see that their Scottish lands be returned to them. There was no point arguing over the issue of succession but there was still time for that. Margaret was certain that the unpopular Elizabeth would slip and get herself arrested in due course for being a heretic.

---

One day, the Lord Chancellor approached the Queen seeking a private audience. But the Queen would not send away her ladies and Margaret stayed by her side.

"You may speak before them," she said, her eyes skimming over letters in her hands.

"Majesty, I have come from the House of Commons. I must put a petition before you that you do not enter into a Spanish alliance, and if you do decide to marry, then let it be an English man who would have English interests at heart." He held out an official document for Mary to take.

A page boy ran forward to accept the letter but Mary stopped him.

"What gives the council such audacity?"

"Bishop Gardiner stands with us on this matter," he said, but the Queen merely pursed her lips tighter.

"In my father's day, God bless him, not one of his councilors would dare make demands of him. Especially not when it came to his marriage."

Margaret flinched at her biting words and was glad she was not on the receiving end of her anger.

"We would not dare presume. We have compiled our report and it is our duty to inform you of popular opinion. The people are not happy. I shall not take up more of your time, your majesty," he said, bowing low and walking backwards without turning his back on her.

Margaret was quick to reassure the Queen.

"You must do what you wish. You cannot always make people happy. Especially in this."

"You are correct, Margaret," Mary replied. "I shall pray on the matter. I would not wish to cause a schism in the realm with my marriage."

"Your gracious majesty, please consider me your most loving, dearest servant. I am yours to command. I offer myself in marriage to you."

Edward Courtney was on his knees before Queen Mary. His cap was off and his hands outstretched to her as though he were praying for deliverance.

Margaret was embarrassed by such a scene. Looking over at the Queen, it was clear she was as well, as the red betraying blush rose up her neck to her cheeks.

"You are kind in your words, but I cannot accept you. Lord Courtney, please rise and do not speak of this again." Her tone as cool as she could muster given the circumstances.

He looked as though he would say something else — perhaps make some claim of her great beauty — again. His eyes looked left and right to the ladies around her and then to Gardiner, who was clearly his backer.

Margaret knew that this young man was now thoroughly embarrassed himself. But how could he have not expected a rejection? Perhaps it was male pride.

Margaret was sure that those lords opposing the Spanish marriage would push for Courtney's suit. He was hardly a political threat and was more than likely to bend to their will. Margaret knew this would suit the councilors well. They chafed at being commanded by a woman who they saw as changeable and weak. They wanted to quell her desire to please the Spaniards too.

It was nearly Christmas before Courtney gave up his suit. He retired from court as gracefully as he could.

Margaret heard with a gleam of amusement that he was visiting Elizabeth at Hatfield often now.

"Do you think he shall try his suit there next?" Margaret joked with her husband, but his expression had turned serious.

"He would do better to retire to his estates and live quietly. At least for a time."

"What do you mean?" Margaret was thinking with mirth at him throwing himself around to see what bride he might catch.

"It is dangerous. It is one thing to play court to the Queen but another to try to capture the attention of the heir. It might look like plotting."

"But this is Edward Courtney, how could anyone suspect him of plotting anything? I'm still half surprised he came out of the Tower with so many courtly manners," Margaret said.

She watched as her husband shrugged his shoulders.

They were happy in these days, but yet she felt he was still on edge. He took his duties as Mary's Master of Hawks diligently and worked hard at befriending all her attendants and the foreign ambassadors. He did not strut around court as though he was full of expectations.

If Margaret was a more cautious person, perhaps she would follow suit, but a few weeks of peace and tranquility had done much for her spirits.

It was Susan Clarencieux, the Mistress of the Robe, who alerted her to trouble.

"Gardiner has been in to see the Queen and he left in a huff," she whispered.

"Do you know what happened?" Margaret asked.

The younger woman shook her head, her fingers touching the prayer beads hanging from her neck, beautiful white pearls.

"Jane Dormer seems to think it is news from Kent. Gardiner has been forbidden from speaking about it. He carried in a petition for Queen Mary."

Margaret bit her lip.

"I shall go in and speak to her," she said, finally deciding on a course of action. "You must speak to the cook tonight, she shall probably want to dine in private."

The lords of the realm were determined not to be ruled by a Queen. They fought Mary's every decision and tried to push their own agendas on her. Margaret walked to the Queen's privy chambers as fast as she could. The swish of her russet gown was the only noise she made.

She found Queen Mary cradling her head in her hands.

"Your grace, you are unwell?" She approached sitting at her feet.

"Just a pain in my head," she said, the weariness evident in her voice.

"Will you tell me what has happened now?" Margaret pressed. "Perhaps I could help you."

"They are so against this marriage."

Margaret knew she was referring to Prince Philip; there was no other marriage for Mary.

"But you have decided. He is a good match," Margaret said, keeping her voice firm.

"Well, now Gardiner warns me of rebellion brewing in the south. I do not have funds or the popularity to defend myself."

"The people love you. They placed you on your throne and God would not abandon you."

"If only the lords would bend to my will. My father never suffered from such disobedient councilors. It is merely the fact that I am a woman that they distrust me. I wish I was married and had a husband that could face them down."

"You shall soon." Margaret hoped she wasn't lying. But she had her deal with the Spanish Ambassador, and she was always encouraging Mary's love of Prince Philip. It was appearing to become a helpless case.

What if the councilors forced another husband on Mary? Would Mary be strong enough to face down a rebellion? In the face of all this uncertainty Margaret had to find the strength to remain steadfast.

She had chosen a side.

Besides, it was not only for selfish reasons that she encouraged this union. Mary's ardor for this man she had never met seemed to grow continuously. She often asked the Spanish Ambassador what the prince would think of this or that. Already it seemed he was shaping national policy.

Margaret wondered what Renard could know of Prince Philip's thoughts but pushed aside her cynicism.

The Christmas season was celebrated with much pomp, and the fighting councilors had to put aside their differences for the time being. The Spanish were given preference, and Queen Mary was forcing her councilors to see what sort of treaty could be agreed upon.

The English were being hard bargainers. They wanted to ensure that England was under no obligation to join the Spanish wars, nor did they want Philip to be regent should anything happen to Queen Mary. They also seemed to complain about the fact that Philip was below in rank to Queen Mary.

The Spanish Ambassador was instructed by the Emperor to be lenient and came to terms with them. The end goal was to see the two of them married. Both the Emperor and the ambassador were sure that, once they were married, Philip could prevail upon Mary to change the terms of the treaty. After all, a husband ruled over his wife, not the other way around.

Margaret was curious to know what Prince Philip thought of the arrangement. He would be a mere consort — not a King — he would gain no political power through this marriage. But hopefully a child would come out of this. A clear Catholic heir that would remove the problem of the Protestant Elizabeth with her dubious heritage.

With the new year, new problems arose.

The Spanish marriage had been announced, but this prompted Kent to rise up in protest. A small rebel army had assembled, but it was more than the Queen could muster at the moment. Even the Duke of Suffolk, the father of Jane Grey, had joined the rebels, but instead of calling for his own daughter to be freed from her prison, he was calling for Lady Elizabeth to be placed on the throne instead of her sister. Margaret wondered if he had gone mad to abandon his child like this.

Many of Mary's loyal adherents were against this Spanish marriage and seemed to make excuses more than anything about why they could not come to her aid.

Margaret was worried. Her husband had departed for the north to arm their tenants and bring them to London to defend the Queen.

Though the court seemed sure that the rebels would not get far, the speed at which they traveled meant that soon they were a mere handful of miles away from London. Some of the London citizens had protested the marriage as well, and now there was worry that they would turn against the Queen. Something had to be done.

Queen Mary was visibly blanched but maintained her cool disposition.

In the meantime, the Lady Elizabeth was summoned to court. At first, she tried to make excuses, but Queen Mary threw off all pretenses and sent an armed retinue to fetch her — giving them permission to use force if necessary. Once Elizabeth was safely tucked away in her rooms at Whitehall Palace, Mary could turn her attention to the pressing issue of the approaching army.

Finally, it was Mary who appealed to the people. She went to the merchant guild hall and gave a bold rousing speech.

Margaret stood behind Queen Mary as she said, "I have come in person to tell you what you already know. I am referring to the traitor army marching towards us. Those Kentish rebels are coming against myself and you, the English people. They claim to be against the Spanish wedding, but this is a mere excuse to cast me off the throne."

She went along in this vein for a while. Her words were clearly touching people's hearts. Margaret could see their hostile expressions soften to ones of caring admiration. By the time she was done they were ready to defend London against the force.

Instead of fleeing, Mary stood firm — the commander at the head of her army. The trust she placed in her people was repaid.

The army appeared before the gates of London and found them shut. Instead of reinforcements and support, they had to face the Tower guns, which were ready to fire on them when they got within range.

They turned and fled — at Ludgate they were stopped and many were arrested. Those who could escaped into the countryside and disappeared back to Kent, but the leaders were not so fortunate.

Thomas Wyatt was brought into the Tower and Queen Mary signed the warrant that named him as a traitor. But she was not done with him. She ordered the Tower guard to torture her prisoner to extract more information out of him. Who was his backer? Who urged him to start this rebellion?

Margaret was stunned by the coldness with which Mary instructed her men.

"I am sure the Lady Elizabeth is implicated in this. Bring me evidence."

"Yes, your grace." The men bowed low, disappearing to do her dirty work.

"Your majesty, are you sure she is involved?" Margaret thought of the Lady Elizabeth dragged away from her home at Hatfield and placed under watch here at court. She was practically a prisoner.

Mary was going down a dark path — not merely trying to get Elizabeth struck out of the succession, but it seemed as though she was seeking her very life. It was with this evil intent that Mary pursued those who she felt betrayed her.

She could be as ruthless as her father had been. This is what Margaret learned in the few days after the rebellion had been squashed.

The Duke of Suffolk was executed, his lands and fortune confiscated by the crown, for he was named as a traitor. His wife fled court and stayed in the singular remaining house to her in London. Her two daughters not imprisoned in the Tower stayed in Queen Mary's train, more demure than usual.

Finally, Queen Mary brought herself to sign the

death warrant for Lady Jane Grey and her husband Guilford.

Matthew walked around with pursed lips, keeping his thoughts to himself. Not even Margaret knew his innermost thoughts, though she could guess at them.

Queen Mary was letting herself be swayed by her council, but it was she that was gaining the blame for all these deaths. Poor Lady Jane Grey, a mere girl, sent to the block for her father's sins.

"May I speak to you in private?" Margaret found herself asking. Her conscience would not let her remain silent.

Queen Mary gazed at her for a moment. "We shall walk in the gardens. It is a pleasant day."

Her retinue followed behind them at a safe distance for Margaret to speak without being overheard.

"I cannot keep myself from asking if there is nothing to be done for the Lady Jane Grey. She is a traitor, but she is also our cousin and so very young. We both know that she had nothing to do with this. She was forced on that throne..."

Margaret trailed off, for Mary was impassive and stiff at her side.

"Of course you are right in your judgement. I just had to ask. I have prayed on it and I found I had to speak to you about it. I must know your mind, your majesty."

"You are a good Christian soul. I know you are tender hearted," Queen Mary said.

Margaret did not correct her. In reality, she had actually been quite happy, imagining every other potential heir being pushed aside in preference of her. She just had been too stupid to realize that they simply wouldn't be crossed off a list — they would have to die first. That was the way. The Tudor way.

"I have decided that if she will convert to the true faith, I will pardon her and send her into exile. I know she herself has not plotted against me, but I won't have her running around as a Protestant heir ready to be snatched up again. Truthfully, it would be safer for me if she was dead. She is young and fertile — a better option for other traitors to use to start a rebellion."

Margaret was taken aback by the frankness with which Mary spoke but also by the hostility.

"I do not want to do this, but they are forcing my hand. I came to this throne without blood being shed. The people wanted me but now already they tire of me. They are ready to rise up against me," Mary continued, a tear escaped from her eyes and trailed down her face. Only Margaret was close enough to see it.

"That is not true. They still love you." Margaret did not add that if Mary did this, her popularity would slip for sure.

Queen Mary gave her a wry smile. "Do not play the courtier now. We have known each other for a very long time. I will pardon her if she cleaves to me. I am not so heartless. My councilors were against me even offering her this option."

"You are wise and I know nothing of ruling a country, nor of the strain it is putting on you. Please let me be of help to you," she said. For she felt bad for Mary being pulled one way or another. She did not command as her father had. Perhaps it was because she was a woman and not a man.

---

A note arrived from Temple Newsham. Matthew came to find her, his pale face warned her that it was bad news.

"Mathieu?"

He grimaced and handed her the hastily written note.

"My Lord, I am writing to you that the doctor has been summoned. Lady Matilda is ill with a fever. At first it was nothing but a slight cough but then she collapsed. We are doing all we can. Please advise if there is anything specific to be done," Margaret read out loud.

Tears sprung into her eyes. Not another baby. Matilda was barely out of her wet clothes. She was going to be two this spring.

"I must go to her immediately!" she declared. "There is nothing here about Darnley. Is he safe?"

"There is no other news."

"Call for my chamberlain," she shouted at a servant standing awkwardly near by. "Go quickly."

Matthew hugged her. "Do not despair. Will you tell the Queen or shall I?"

"I will go." She wiped her eyes. "You are right. Children are ill all the time. I will go and nurse her back to health."

Queen Mary gave her permission to be away from

court, and so she wasn't around to witness the confusion that followed.

Lady Jane Grey defied all expectations. She did not jump at the chance to be pardoned by converting to the Catholic faith. Instead, she argued with the priests Mary sent to convince her and stood firm. She would not betray her beliefs. She would not sacrifice her eternal soul for temporary comforts.

Margaret would have been shocked, but her time was spent trying to heal the little creature in her arms. She was holding her tightly as the little girl dug her hands into her hair and snuffled at the nape of her neck as if she was a baby once again.

It broke her heart.

Day after day, she did not improve. Her pallor seemed to get paler, and she was noticeably weaker.

Queen Mary even sent her own physician to look at her.

"Is there nothing that can be done?" Margaret was trying to hold back the tears as she questioned him in the hall outside the nursery.

"I am afraid not. Only God's intervention will save this child. I am so very sorry."

She had her maid write to Matthew to come home as quickly as he could.

She resolved never to leave her child's side. She brought in her prie-dieu, and when she was not tending to Matilda, she was praying. She also paid for prayers to be said at their church. Anything to save her.

# CHAPTER 7

## 1554-1555

As SHE WAS WATCHING the little coffin being placed into the ground in London, her cousin Lady Jane Grey lost her head. Matthew by her side led her away as the priest finished saying the words.

"I cannot bear it," she sobbed. "I cannot bear another loss."

"You did all you could. I should have come with you."

Margaret could hear the guilt in his own words, and she comforted him in return. "You are the very best of fathers. She knows you loved her. She is with God now."

"You must eat something tonight," he ordered, refusing to allow himself to be reassured. "You are wasting away."

They spent two weeks tucked away in Temple Newsham playing with their son, comforting each other and letting the world slip away. But they had responsibilities that could not wait any longer. It was with a heavy heart that they packed away their clothes and prepared for the journey back to London.

"Can I not go with you?" Darnley was sitting in her lap as though he was a little boy, examining the gold chain that hung about her neck.

"No, you shall stay here and continue your lessons. But I shall have your father send you a new horse for you are outgrowing your pony. What color shall you like?" She smiled at him.

"Black!" he said. "No, a grey one like father's."

"As you wish." She ruffled his hair.

"I need new riding boots as well," he said. "I want gold buckles on them, not just the silver ones I have now."

"You can have them when you are older."

"No, now." His face scrunched up looking as though he was going to cry.

Margaret frowned at him. "At the very least, you can ask me politely and mind your manners, or have your tutors been neglectful?"

He shot her a grin and jumped from her lap.

"My dear lady mother, may I please have a pair of new riding boots with gold buckles and spurs?"

"Much better," she said, giving him an appraising look.

"So may I?"

"Yes, I shall send them from London. Now give me a kiss and go off to bed."

He did as he was ordered. "I love you, Mama."

It warmed her heart to hear him say that. "I love you as well. Be a good boy and may God bless you."

Of course, Matthew scolded her for indulging his every whim.

"Think of the expense. The boy will outgrow them in a season and he will need a fresh pair."

"He deserves the very best. Besides we can afford it now."

"You indulge him, I indulge you. Pray we never end up on the street because of it."

"I shall every night," she teased. They both laughed, the first time in weeks that they had done so.

The court was frantic with preparations for the Queen's wedding. No one seemed to be talking about the poor Lady Jane Grey. She was all but forgotten.

Margaret took warning from this and knew that her cousin the Queen would not flinch again from executing those in her way.

Perhaps bloodthirst ran in Mary's Tudor blood.

The decision was not popular with the people, though they understood the reasons why. But they no longer saw Mary as the poor innocent princess who was exiled by her father. Now she was just as tainted.

Her councilors were happier and more at ease. Margaret could see their self-satisfied strutting. Gardiner, appointed Lord Chancellor, was still pressing for Mary to proceed against Elizabeth, but there was no concrete proof to be found.

Mary was wary of executing her sister on false

charges. She was popular and she dared not risk another uprising.

"Do you really think they would rise for her?" Margaret asked, surprised to discover this real threat.

"My sister has not been idle," Queen Mary said, nipping off the thread with her teeth. They were working on embroidering a tapestry. "She has thrust herself in the public's eye with her charity and traveling from house to house, greeting the peasants and gentry on the way. It helps she is young and pretty. I don't think many would bother to consider that she's only a little better than a heretic."

The spite in her voice as she mentioned her sister's prettiness told Margaret of her jealousy. King Henry could never stand to be overshadowed either.

"What shall you do with her then?"

"I shall send her under guard to the country. A loyal gentleman shall be her jailer," she said.

So the plans were already under way. It had been decided. Margaret could see the benefit of this for herself. She would be the first lady at court after the Queen.

"Let us speak of something else," Mary all but commanded.

"Of course, I apologize for bringing it up. Have you heard any more news from the Spanish Ambassador?"

Mary blushed at this. "Prince Philip has been crowned King of Naples and his father has made him King of Jerusalem as well. In short, he is preparing to come to marry me as soon as he can."

"Is he displeased that the English Parliament won't crown him?"

"I am sure he was disappointed at first," she replied with a frown which told Margaret she was unsure.

"It will be such a merry time when he arrives with his retinue. I am sure the people will rejoice."

"Yes, I have arranged for several pageants and feasts to be prepared. I heard he also likes masquerades. We shall show him that England can be a wonderful home for him."

"When he arrives he shall never want to leave your side," Margaret said with some sincerity. Why would he wish to run off? Though perhaps he wouldn't take it kindly to be saddled with an aging wife. But in the weeks following her return to court, Margaret noticed that as the date for her marriage approached, Queen Mary was looking more and more happy. Her skin glowed and she carried herself with more confidence.

She was anticipating having someone to share the burden of governing with not to mention that this was her chance to be loved.

Margaret had been around for previous interviews with the Spanish Ambassadors and she felt he had been laying it on quite thick. Did he not realize that if Philip's love for Mary was indeed so ardent then he would have written to her in person already? He might have even appeared sooner for a visit before the wedding.

Still she remained a staunch supporter of the Spanish marriage. She had her own interests to think of and Mary was keen on it. Her support only made her cousin's estimation of her grow.

---

It was done. It was over with. The Queen was wedded and bedded. She was retreating from court to be with her new husband for two days and had taken a small party out hunting.

Margaret was feeling unwell. A spasm in her back kept her indoors much to her displeasure at missing out.

King Philip had arrived with a large group of Spanish retainers. This irked the English nobility for now there weren't as many spots for them to fill in his household. It seemed as though he thought they weren't good enough to serve him.

Philip had been used to larger households running more formally, so he had not considered this nor had his ambassador warned him. He tried correcting this misstep by assuring everyone that many of the Spanish who arrived with him would be returning home after the wedding.

In the meantime, Margaret and the other ladies were treated to fresh faces at court.

The Spanish men were surprised by what they saw as brazen women. In Spain, women were more conservative and refrained from participating in court activities like dancing. To the English women, the Spaniards were alluring with their fancy clothes and enticing accents.

There was a great show of interest on both sides.

What Margaret wondered was how the King felt about his new wife. She knew from Mary's own mouth that she was smitten with her new husband and prayed to God each morning that she might conceive a child.

Outwardly, he was polite.

Margaret felt this was a strained politeness. The type of politeness she used to give to her elders knowing she had to please them. But whatever she might suspect or he might tell his closest companions, he was nothing but pleasant to the Queen. She glowed under his attention.

"We should visit Darnley at Temple Newsham when the court moves to Hampton Court," her husband said one evening.

"I would dearly love that. It has been too long. Do you think the Queen will give me leave?"

"I have spoken to her when she rode out hunting this morning," he said with a tender kiss on her brow. "The court feels overcrowded."

"Are you suggesting we won't be missed if we go?" Margaret accused him.

"No, not at all. But I dearly wish to see our son and get a break from the court," he said, weariness creeping into his voice.

"What is wrong? Should we all not be happy now that she is married?"

"You may not know this but the lords are fighting again. King Philip is asking for military support — something the treaty specifically forbade. He says it is her duty as his wife to obey him. She agreed to ask but warned him the answer was likely to be no. The harvests have been bad this year and the coffers are all but empty."

Margaret shook her head at all this information.

"I had not heard."

"I heard it from Sir William Cecil. He works as a secretary for her majesty. He is a smart man," he said. "Young but quick and level-headed."

"As opposed to others who serve the Queen?" Margaret teased but he nodded.

"Most of her councilors fight amongst themselves rather than helping the Queen and country to improve. It's chaotic."

"Like who?"

"Well for example, we have Cardinal Pole and Bishop Gardiner are at each other's throats on how to take the Church of England forward."

"Everything was decided, wasn't it?"

"They are bickering over the schematics. Anyways, at the very least the English people will not have to give back the lands they bought from the dissolution of the monasteries. That would have led to uprisings for sure. The Cardinal wants to flush out heretics, but Gardiner is not so keen on bringing the inquisition to England."

"It will settle down." Margaret thought of how long it took whenever a new ruler came to the throne, before the jockeying for power and position stopped. "They will fight it out and then, once the new order of things is established, all will be well."

"I am glad to see you are so optimistic," he said. "After the Queen's entrance into London, we shall depart and you shall have some work of your own to conduct in the country if I am not mistaken."

She gleamed up at him. "Counting the weeks?" Her belly was round and she was carrying high — a sure sign of a healthy baby boy.

"I want both of you to be well but it is also time now that Darnley took his lessons more seriously. I am hiring a tutor for him, and I wish to oversee his transition from the nursery to the school room."

"He is growing so handsome. Time is passing by too quickly."

"I feel the same," he said, a far off look on his face. He seemed weary once more.

---

Margaret became the Queen's Keeper of the Privy Purse. It was now in her power to pay fees and distribute goods and charity. Yet again, her star was rising, but she found it did not bring her much joy.

She longed to leave for Temple Newsham. The pageantry of a new court welcoming its King was overtaxing. Being on her feet all day and most of the night was leaving her exhausted to the point she was barely tasting the food on her plate.

It was with relief that she rode with Matthew to the north. A large train of retainers following after them with their goods.

Margaret was overjoyed to see her son, his blonde curls just as soft as when he was a babe. He bowed for her blessing but then hugged her. She laughed at his formality and then the ease with which he slipped into the role of being a child again.

"Have you brought me presents, lady mother?"

"Many. I shall show them once they have been unpacked."

"And a new horse? I haven't forgotten I wanted a new horse," he said with a pout.

She should have scolded him for his impatience, and his father seemed to think so as well. But Matthew did nothing more than look disapprovingly at him. Darnley had the good sense to look down as though ashamed.

"We have brought you a new horse. You can see him after dinner. If you behave and if I have heard that you have been studying well," she tempered.

"Oh, I have been!"

"That's good to know," Matthew said, studying him. "It is important you apply yourself. Now run to your rooms — we must rest from our journey."

He sped off to obey.

"He shall make a good courtier."

"How so?" Margaret asked, turning to her husband.

"He asks and asks and is never satisfied," he chuckled.

"He knows his worth."

"We spoil him," he corrected.

They stayed until August. The baby arrived early. A strong little boy they baptized Philip in honor of the King. Queen Mary sent her blessings along with jewels and a gold cup for the baby. Among the gifts was a message for Margaret to return to court as soon as she was able.

"What do you make of this summons?"

"She misses your company," her husband said, looking over the letter.

"I don't know why I am reading into it too much. It must be good news though." Mary never usually used such flowery language and would not have bothered if it had been bad news.

"Well, the baby is doing well with the nursemaid and you shall be churched soon. I can begin making preparations to go back to London."

"Very well," Margaret said. Realizing suddenly that she would have to leave her children again. "By the way, I have written to Hans Eworth to commission a painting of Darnley."

"How extravagant of you," he chided her, but he did so in a childish way that let her know he wasn't upset by the idea. "Perhaps we can have a copy given to Queen Mary as a gift. She is so fond of him."

"Yes, and it would remind her of him." Margaret trailed off, not wishing to finish the thought that might lead her into treason and greed.

With Darnley learning Latin and French with John Elder, Margaret and Matthew set off for London. Their progress slower and less enthusiastic than on their trip to Temple Newsham.

The court had been merry and had gone on a mini progress around London in their absence. They did not travel far south or north but stayed near the city. Margaret was surprised that Mary would not have wanted to go all the way to York or even Ludlow since she was so loved by the people there and had pleasant memories.

She soon discovered the secret when Queen Mary invited her to pray with her in her private chapel.

"Margaret, I have missed my course twice," Mary said under her breath.

"You have?" Margaret's first thought was that Mary had begun her change of life.

Seeing the worry in her face Mary turned to her. "I believe I am with child."

"Oh! My dear Mary — I mean, your majesty. Congratulations!" She wanted to hug her but wasn't sure if that was proper, so she stood back and merely grasped her hand.

"I have only told my suspicions to King Philip and to you. I shall wait another month and then consult with a midwife, but I am sure the court is already suspicious. It has been nearly three months and I have not bled," she whispered.

"And you are ill in the mornings?"

"Sometimes I am ill all day."

Margaret nodded. "It is like that sometimes. I shall pray for you every day and night. My dearest cousin, I am so happy for you."

"Thank you." Mary squeezed her hand right back. "I pray I shall deliver England the Catholic prince it needs."

"Amen," Margaret said devoutly.

But in her secret heart, she felt a slight twinge of disappointment that now she would be set aside — her chances at the throne lost.

# CHAPTER 8

1555

IN THE LATE SPRING, Queen Mary retreated from the world to await the birth of the prince everyone said must come. King Philip had bid his wife a kind farewell. It was done with more emotion than one might think.

Philip had been at odds with Mary lately, but now their goals were united on this one important thing. Whatever child Mary carried in her belly — if it lived — would be the heir to the great Spanish Empire and to England.

This child would unite two nations.

Margaret knew well that many of the Protestant lords were on their knees praying every night that the child would not live or even that both mother and child would perish during this dangerous time. They were being hounded by the Catholic Bishops. Heretics were being rounded up and burned at the stake. Lands and goods were confiscated, and those who had not fled in the early days of Mary's reign now found themselves trapped.

Margaret did not pity them. During Edward's reign, it was people like her that got hounded to their deaths. Queen Mary was only doing what she thought was right.

The first signs of trouble came when the Queen's due date came and went.

"You might have been mistaken about the date," Jane Dormer said.

"I might have been."

Margaret looked at Queen Mary who was sitting straight backed in her chair, a hand to her bulging belly. Margaret shared a look with Jane Dormer, they both knew that the Queen was not a fool to not be able to count the days.

"Shall I call for the physicians to examine you?" Margaret asked.

Mary waved in ascent and they were summoned.

They did not step into the darkened room of confinement. No man could enter until the child was born and this was not a court to break with convention. Instead the doctors in their dark cloaks waited outside the screen door and passed along questions to a maid who repeated them to the Queen and carried back her answers to them.

"Do you feel the child sitting lower now, your grace?"

"Do you feel tired during the day but awake at night, your majesty?"

The questions went on for quite some time, then the physicians deliberated.

"There was a miscounting of dates. There are no signs that labor would begin shortly, but perhaps in another two weeks to four weeks time," one had said.

Margaret herself was a bit incredulous, but it was not impossible that Mary had been so mistaken.

The Queen's foolishness and inability to count was more plausible to these learned men than the fact that something else might be wrong. It was accepted readily by everyone. Never mind that Mary had the best tutors growing up and that she had waited so anxiously for this day.

This endless waiting went on and on.

Finally, in late July her stomach began receding. It was not noticeable at first, but by August there was no doubt that the Queen was not with child.

Her stomach shrank back to its normal size.

In those last desperate days before she had to face the court, she did not eat and would only take sips of wine. She was on her knees praying. None of her ladies, not even Margaret, could imagine what she was saying to the God on whom she had always relied on.

They left the closed off rooms without ceremony. Margaret was glad to be out of the rooms which now stank of stale air and sweat. They had not been properly cleaned in months. Fresh herbs could only do so much.

She attended mass with the Queen in the chapel royal. The courtiers who had been waiting for months for the birth of the heir looked at her with a combination of pity and irritation.

The King was cold to his returning wife.

"Madame." He offered her his arm without so much as a glance at her.

Margaret watched as Mary hesitated, her eyes searched his face for some sort of acknowledgment, but finding none, she steeled herself and entwined her arm around his. They could all feel that he was furious. He felt that she had made him a laughing stock in Europe. That Mary had made herself into one as well.

English pride was hurt. Margaret doubted that this would ever be forgotten.

At dinner, she was seated below the dais where the King and Queen dined under the canopy of estate. She heard the King ask if Mary would support him with English troops in Flanders. Margaret thought she would not dare refuse him at such a time, but to her surprise, Mary held firm.

"Then I must tell you that I must depart for Flanders as soon as I can. The war against the French is going badly there. I am needed," he said.

"You are needed here."

"I will not stay here to bow to my wife's commands. I will not stay here to be a powerless fool. Already I have delayed my going, and for nothing."

The cold reproach even made Margaret cringe at the heartlessness of the words. Her cousin's heart must be breaking beyond belief, but she could not turn her head to see lest she alert them to the fact she had heard.

Truth be told, many had heard the King reproach his wife. Even a Queen was not set above her husband.

Whatever fury or hurt the Queen felt towards him, she never let him see it. She treated him as lovingly as ever and tried to persuade him to stay. They could try again. She did not have many fertile years ahead of her, but they could still try to have a child.

Philip of Spain could not be turned from his path, and Margaret was in the Queen's train as they bid him and his Spanish escort farewell.

She wondered if he would ever return to England. After all, the English had not greeted him kindly. There was not much here for him except for an aging disagreeable wife and the long wet months that inevitably led to bad harvests and hunger.

They were walking in the garden like a pair of young lovers, hand clasped and heads together. Margaret commented on this to Matthew who laughed.

"And are we not in love?"

"I am sure many would see it as obscene that we love each other so openly," she said.

"Imagine what they would say if I kissed you here and now."

She looked up at him then and saw the mischief in his face.

"Renard approached me after dinner." Matthew turned the conversation to more serious matters. "It seems that now is the time for us to press for our suit in Scotland. You for your lands and me for mine. I shall write to Mary de Guise and send my man Laurence Nesbit to France."

"It is all decided then?"

He must have sensed the irritation in her voice at the name Mary de Guise. He had been pursuing her suit before deciding on marrying Margaret. This was something she never forgot. He never spoke of her, of course, but Margaret never liked thinking she was merely the second choice. It hurt her pride.

"It is within her power to grant us our land back and persuade the Scottish lords to pardon me. Renard says Queen Mary has written to the Scottish council asking them to work with us. This was at Philip's suggestion."

"Some payment then for my loyal service," Margaret said. She felt the guilt at having encouraged her cousin into this marriage that led her to such unhappiness.

"Have you been conspiring with the Spanish, my love? They aren't well loved by the English people, you know," he said.

"I don't need to be reminded. It was not me that led to this, but I wonder every day how she pressed on with the marriage in the face of such hatred from the people." She looked around to make sure they were quite alone.

"Treason now?"

"I know you are joking, but she is more than happy to burn heretics at the stake. She is turning cold like my uncle. Unhappiness has drained the mercy out of her."

Beside her, Matthew pulled her closed as though to hug her.

"Do not dwell on it. God must be unhappy with England indeed if he continues to send these rains to us. The people are hungry and the Queen can think of nothing else that might be causing God's wrath to come upon us."

She could barely hear his words. She knew that he had been converted by the Protestants but as ever had turned his coat back to Catholicism as soon as he saw the tide turn. He was a survivor. He would keep his beliefs close to his heart and not tell anyone, not even her what he truly felt. She could merely suspect, for he did not pray as ardently under the Catholic Mass as he had the Protestant.

Queen Mary was often in meetings with her council. She was urging them at Philip's request to join the war against France. She did this only half-heartedly, for she was in a rebellious mood now that he had abandoned her to face the angry English lords.

In contrast to her pale aging sister, Princess Elizabeth was shining. She rode out every day with a train of ladies and gentlemen attending her. She went hawking and hunting and in the evenings she danced and played cards long into the night.

To Mary it was like she was rubbing her youth and vitality in her face. The Queen could barely stand to face her sister and rarely said more than two words to her.

Margaret, remembering keenly that she had not treated Elizabeth kindly when she had been imprisoned under suspicion, tried to act kinder to her but kept by Mary's side. She had the pride of a woman past her best years and refused to stand beside the glowing princess to be compared.

Queen Mary sequestered herself more and more inside her palace. Outside the people were terrified and had come to hate her.

The smell of burning flesh seemed to fill the city air, and there was nothing to show for it. England was not cleansed of heretics, and God was not smiling down upon these acts.

The harvests were still failing, the weather was cold and wet. The King had abandoned his wife, and now they would get no heir from the Queen. They became bitter and defiant. Would the Queen stop at nothing until the whole country was burned?

After this summer of anxiety, Margaret discovered she was pregnant. She said nothing to the Queen, but as her belly grew obscenely big, she could no longer put it off.

"Your majesty, I shall have to ask you to excuse me in March for I am with child and will retreat to Temple Newsham for my lying in," she said, keeping her head downcast.

"A baby?" Mary coughed to hide her statement. "Congratulations, dearest cousin. We shall have to pray you will come out of your confinement in good health. You and the baby."

"Thank you, your grace." Margaret swept her a deep curtsey. "I should rather have stayed with you through Lent."

"Perhaps my husband shall return by then, and I shall be too preoccupied to notice your absence," she said.

"He is returning?" Margaret was hopeful that now the Queen might find some cheer.

"He writes to me that he shall soon but cannot yet settle on a date. The ambassador assures me that he shall come."

"Please God he does." Margaret grasped Mary's hands and kissed them. "I pray that you too shall be brought to bed with a baby of your own."

She said this by way of apology for her own condition. Indeed, if Margaret was still able to conceive at her great age, why not Mary as well?

---

Her husband would escort her home and then return to court. They had heard of some promise to gain a castle in Scotland. Mary de Guise's response had been promising, and the castle of Tantallon was in her power to give back to them. It could be their foothold.

"Can you not stay with me?" Margaret asked, she was weary with this child that she carried so heavy in her belly. "I shall be miserable without you."

"It is best I go, but I shall return to celebrate Easter with you and the birth of our child," he promised.

Margaret could not find words to keep him with her.

"Very well," she said.

"I promise I shall make it up to you with a great many gifts this holiday season. So be of good cheer, Maggie."

"Only if there will be indeed a great many gifts."

"Ah, the Tudor greed shines forth. Careful, sweetheart."

But she laughed, pushing him away. She was far from being a naive child.

They traveled as fast as possible, not wishing to spend more time on the road than necessary.

The previous wet summer had led to a bad harvest and there was hunger in the country. Margaret did not pull back the curtains of her litter to let the cool spring air flow in or to look at the people gathered on the side of the road. Besides, there was no cheering to be heard. In a particularly bad hamlet they rode through, she instructed her treasurer to hand out some coin to the people who looked wretched and thinner than the rest. To some children with gaunt faces she sent her breakfast.

They did not linger though, fearing sickness might be running rampant through this part of the county as well as poverty.

By the time they arrived at Temple Newsham, Margaret was weary. She took to her bed and remained there for several days.

Darnley and Philip were brought to her with all due haste. Philip complained bitterly about being forced to wear his finest and as it happened most comfortable jacket.

"I cannot play mama," he said.

"You look very handsome. You cannot always be running around like a child. You shall have to grow up and join your brother in the school room. Your brother does not complain."

At this praise, Darnley puffed out his chest.

"Is father coming too? I want him to show me how to joust and duel with a sword!"

"You don't want to learn to shoot?"

"None of the Knights in my stories used gunpowder. It is not the chivalrous way."

"You'd know best," she said, smiling at him with indulgence. She did not correct him that the days of Knights in shining armor riding off to battle were long over.

---

King Philip had returned to be with Mary but his visit had been brief. He was curt with her, requiring the support of the English army against the French. It did not matter to him that the country was ill equipped for war. But with some convincing, the council and his wife finally gave him what he wanted.

Many volunteered for the army, imagining gaining rich spoils from France.

It was a disaster, of course. Beyond all belief, England lost Calais — their last foothold in France. It was her husband that brought her this grave news.

"There is more to add than this loss. We will not gain anything in Scotland," he said.

Margaret propped herself up on her elbows. Her big belly before her.

"So it was hopeless? We've bribed every man on the council."

"Don't trouble yourself. Think of the baby and it is never hopeless. We shall persevere and live to fight another day. I shall never give up the fight."

"That's true," she said and rested again against her pillow.

"Darnley deserves his inheritance and Philip should be left something too. We are part of the royal family and by all rights should be part of two royal families — Scotland and England."

"Yes, darling."

She knew from his tone he was patronizing her and she glared up at him.

"Darnley is looking well and Philip has grown so much." He quickly changed the topic of conversation.

And so she was pulled into a long discussion about their children, the many plans and schemes she had for them.

This new baby was long in coming. She missed the May Day celebrations. Matthew, as sweet as when they had first been married, had singers posted beneath the windows of her lying in chambers and they serenaded her for all the morning. It lifted her spirits to hear the music, though she could not go outside nor pull back the heavy tapestries covering the windows.

She emerged from the birthing chamber in a victorious mood. Her third son, a bonny boy with blonde curls, who would be christened Charles in honor of King Philip's father. She received congratulations and gifts from all quarters of the realm. Even the Spanish Ambassador sent her a kind note along with a rosary for the infant.

Though she felt rounder, she felt reinvigorated with the birth of yet another son. Of all the Tudors, she seemed the most blessed and fecund. Yes, she had lost children, but with three sons in her nursery, what more could she ask for? What more could prove God's favor?

She did not return to court until August for the Queen was not going on progress — she believed she was pregnant and so did not wish to travel. She had already stayed away as long as she dared. As much as Margaret loved her children, she knew that for their benefit she had to be at court. She was not part of a private family that might live out their days in the country. She also wondered at the futility of going.

Margaret, not wishing to appear disloyal, kept her doubts in regards to the Queen's pregnancy to herself and did not even voice them to her husband.

Upon entering the Queen's privy chambers, she greeted her cousin with much felicity and accepted congratulations in return.

They passed much of the time stitching shirts for the poor, hearing one or another of the ladies reading from good Christian books and occasionally walking around the grounds when weather permitted.

As summer gave way to autumn, the doctors knew it

was time to talk to the Queen. Though at first her stomach had ballooned out and she had been experiencing pain as well as a cessation of her monthly courses, nothing about her now seemed to indicate a pregnancy. She was pale, barely ate, and her stomach had not changed its shape. Additionally, by this time, she should have felt the baby quicken, and as the child had not moved, it was either another false pregnancy or it had died.

This was a delicate subject that they weren't sure how to broach with the Queen. She seemed oblivious to this and was proceeding with plans for her confinement. The business of government was set aside, and she was penning urgent letters to her husband to recall him from Flanders.

To these pleas he ignored her but promised he would return after the birth of his child and wished her well. Margaret knew by this that he doubted his wife as well.

Everyone seemed certain that Mary was not pregnant except for Mary herself.

The doctors approached her ladies, pleading with them one by one to speak to the Queen, but many either crossed themselves and walked away or refused as a matter of principle.

The Queen would not thank the messenger for this news.

"My lady, you must speak to her. At least let her give us permission to examine her. If there is a tumor present or a dead baby we must know. To delay could be fatal."

Margaret, grim faced but resolute, nodded in agreement. "I promise you sirs that I shall speak to her after mass tomorrow. but I cannot promise anything."

They nodded relieved and bowed to her. Margaret would have to take things in hand, since the others seemed incapable or too scared.

As they walked back from the chapel, Margaret took Mary's hands in hers and pressed her to listen to what she had to say.

"I am your cousin and I love you, your grace. I have nothing but your best wishes at heart. Please let the physicians examine you. I pray for nothing else that this child of yours shall be born healthy and strong but..."

"But what?" the Queen interrupted.

"But you do not look well. No one will speak for fear of offending you, but I can only think of your well being," Margaret said rather bluntly.

Seeing her cousins shoulders droop told Margaret that she had won.

"It might only be a mistake of the days."

The old excuse that had been repeated over and over last time made Margaret shrink away from her.

"No, this time I am quite certain."

"Of course, your majesty," Margaret said with a curtsey.

The Queen walked off without waiting for her to rise and Margaret thought it would be best not to go after her. The Spanish Ambassador caught her eye and he nodded at her. Everyone was happy except for the Queen and herself, who had to bear the brunt of the Queen's disappointment.

Indeed, in the days following, the Queen acted coldly towards her. When she needed someone to read to her, she asked Jane Dormer or another of her ladies. She no longer invited Margaret into her confidence. This coldness continued until she was summoned into her rooms a week later.

The Queen was crying into her pillows. Her sobs were mostly muffled but Margaret felt her heart break at such a sad sight. This was not the stately woman she saw walking up to her throne in Westminster Abbey just a few years ago. This was a disappointed woman made tiny and ill by the many sorrows that plagued her life.

"Mary," she said running to her side, dropping all formality. "Please, tell me you are well."

"How could God have betrayed me like this?"

"He has not."

"Why has He taken away yet another child from me? And my husband, where is he? Have I not tried my best to rid England of the heretics? Have I not been a good wife?"

Margaret bit her tongue and, in a moment, wrapped her arms around her cousin in a tight embrace.

Mary must have steadied herself, for she appeared at dinner straight faced, laced tightly in a luxurious gown of black taffeta.

Margaret was at her side, a glare ready for anyone who dared comment or even so much as give the Queen a side glance. She would be her defender, her shield. She knew behind the Queen's back, everyone was whispering that she had failed to give England an heir yet again.

The Catholics at court were visibly worried — for the next Catholic heir was Mary of Scots, but she had been eliminated from the succession. They seemed to treat Margaret and her husband with more deference, but it was to Elizabeth that everyone looked.

Indeed this preening bastard turned princess again was in high spirits. She had the favor of the Spanish King that kept her sister's anger at bay, and she seemed to flaunt her health and good fortune in her aging sister's face. By all accounts, she would be the next heir but everyone knew of her Protestant tendencies. Would she turn back the clock yet again? Would she begin burning Catholics as heretics just as Queen Mary was doing to the Protestants?

Margaret gave up trying to press Mary to name her successor instead of Elizabeth. She was the clear favorite and she knew Elizabeth had been wily enough to gather support around her. It was not only the support of the old Protestant lords that flocked to her, but even foreign aid from the French had been promised.

Her husband had even said that the Spanish Ambassador had been visiting her in secret.

It was clear then that Margaret would have to set aside her dislike for Elizabeth and prepare herself to serve her as she had served Mary.

When Elizabeth requested of Mary that she return to Hatfield for her health, Queen Mary did not even hesitate to give her permission.

"I am glad to be free of her," Mary said in private to Margaret one evening. "I couldn't stand her obstinance."

"She enjoyed showing off," Margaret agreed.

"She was setting up a rival court beneath my very nose. It is better she is at Hatfield where I cannot see how she betrays me every day with her words and deeds. She should be cleaving to me."

Before Mary could work herself into a fit of anger, Margaret changed the subject.

"And what did the Spanish Ambassador say? Has he news of King Philip?"

"He says he is well and that he sends his regards. I wish he would come to England. It is not his regards I wish for but his presence. I fear I have lost him forever now."

"He loves you."

"He loves me so much that he stays away? Loves me so much that he takes up with other women? At least he would not dare divorce me, or I would be like my dear miserable mother. Dead of a broken heart," Mary said, a hand resting on her belly. She grimaced.

"Are you feeling unwell?" Margaret asked concerned. Lately, she had often noticed the Queen doing this.

"A pain in my belly, the doctors are investigating but it seems the tumor in my belly grows and shrinks with each passing week. I fear I am unwell and nothing but God's miracle and blessing are keeping me on my feet."

Margaret glanced around but the other ladies were talking amongst themselves and none seemed to have overheard this melancholy thought.

"There must be something that can be done for you, your grace."

Mary gave her a weary smile. "I fear that I shall not live to see another Christmas season and that this Kingdom shall fall once again into ruin. I wish I could have given you what you desired and made you my heir. I know you at least would have kept England in the faith."

"Do not say that. Please." Margaret felt tears prickling at the corner of her eyes.

It terrified her to see what new lows women could be brought to. Even as a Queen, Mary was all but powerless.

They had been young women together and now Margaret felt as though she had been eclipsed by Elizabeth. As if overnight she had become an aging woman, but at least she was loved by her husband and had three wonderful sons around her.

What did Mary have but ill health and a traitorous sister?

With Mary ill all summer, as she was visibly getting weaker by the day, the courtiers began drifting away. Some went to their homes, but a great many went to Hatfield. Reports said Elizabeth was gathering many attendants around her. They hunted during the day and made merry all night.

Margaret walked around the Queen's rooms with irritation evident on her face. She was quick to snap at a clumsy maid.

The ambitious part of her wanted to go to Hatfield as well — the part that wanted to ingratiate herself with the new apparent ruler of England. But the other prideful part refused to play court to Elizabeth. Lastly was her love for Mary, which had grown stronger in these last few weeks.

Mary was flawed — she could be as ruthless as any Tudor, but she had lived a difficult life. They had shared many of their younger years together. Margaret knew how much Mary had suffered for her beliefs, and it seemed cruel for God to have rewarded her so poorly. She neither had a child nor husband to dote on. No one seemed to care much for her. Even Margaret cursed herself for her desire to be freed from this dull court that waited for Mary to die.

King Philip did not write to his ailing wife. That, perhaps, was the most tragic thing.

Every day the ambassador promised the Queen of his love and devotion to her. Saying that he was praying for her return to health and that perhaps, in the new year, he would return to England.

Margaret watched the ambassador carefully and knew that some of what he said was a lie. She doubted King Philip thought much of his wife. Like everyone, his attentions were now on Elizabeth.

"Do you think she would marry him?" Mary asked her one evening as they sat before the fire with Margaret plaiting her hair.

"I do not think she would," she said after a long pause.

"A pity."

Margaret was surprised and exclaimed aloud.

"It is true. If she married him — traitorous though it

would be, then England would be maintained in the true faith. And then she would eventually see how I am suffering, for he will disappoint whatever woman he marries after me."

Margaret continued her work in silence, grinding her teeth to keep silent.

"I want her to suffer the heartache I am now feeling. I want her to feel just as utterly alone as I am. Then perhaps she will think more tenderly of me. We should have been loving sisters to one another but instead we've been at each other's throats," Mary said.

To Margaret she sounded remorseful.

"Please don't speak like this. You know I am here — loyal to you and you may yet recover. The doctors are optimistic that the spring may return your good spirits."

She didn't know what else to say, and as she finished plaiting her hair, she offered to read to her.

"Not tonight, Margaret. Good night — I wish to be alone now."

Margaret curtseyed and left the chamber. Hoping Jane or Susan would stay with her through the night. She went to find her husband, needing to clear her own head and make plans for the future.

He was busy writing letters when she approached.

"Are you to become a secretary?" she said.

He greeted her with a warm smile. "If you felt it was necessary. But no, I am sorting out some things and responding to letters I have put off for too long. Did you need me?"

"The Queen is unwell."

This was not news but it felt more final when she said it out loud. As if up until now they had all been pretending that this was nothing serious.

"More than that, she fears she will…" Margaret bit off her words but her husband knew what she was going to say. Everyone was thinking it.

"Do you think Elizabeth will throw out the Catholics for the Protestants?"

Such treasonous talk made Margaret shift uneasily as she stood before him.

"It is you who must have some idea." Margaret stole a glance at his papers. "You are always talking to Cecil. I am just trying to care for the Queen."

"I think we shall have to be flexible as we have been all our lives. We shall become loving cousins once again to the future monarch. We are fortunate you are so well connected."

"I have never been so kind nor friendly to Elizabeth," Margaret said, though it pained her to admit this for it showed that she had acted foolishly.

"I daresay many have not been so kind to her. Your actions will be forgotten and you will be perfect friends. Do not even mention the past."

Margaret couldn't help but scoff as if she would be such a fool.

"Sometimes I wish for nothing more than to retire from the court and all its intrigues. I wish to make Temple Newsham our permanent home and live out the rest of my life in comfort and seclusion."

"You would wish for that?"

Margaret smiled, suddenly deep in thought. At length she replied. "No, I think it would drive me insane. But I do wish I knew where I stood. It always seems I am fighting for a place and for favor. I wish to be certain. It is only you that I am certain of."

"Life is nothing but uncertainty. But let us not fall into philosophical discussions. Our battle continues, whereas Queen Mary is readying herself to leave it. We must not linger on bygones but look to the future."

"You speak so assuredly."

"One way or another, I feel it is clear that Elizabeth is the heir. I cannot know how long it will be until she will claim her inheritance, nor would I wish to speculate." They both thought of the men dead on the scaffold for drawing up the Queen's astrology charts, trying to determine the date of her death. "We must prepare to play a new role."

They spoke thus, in half-riddles, well into the night. Matthew's letters lay unwritten until the morning. Margaret had to try to be of good cheer when she returned to the Queen's rooms.

---

Without realizing it, she had said goodbye to her cousin and now it was as if she was serving a ghost. In truth there was little left in this shell of a woman that she could have recognized. This woman was weak and tired, barely speaking, absorbed in the Latin words of the mass.

Weeks went on like this and many wondered if this is how it would be for years to come. A sickly Queen and an inert government. The people were chafing unhappily at their circumstances, but they were too hungry or weary to do anything about it. If there had not been years of failed harvests, perhaps they would have risen up in rebellion.

With the cold weather came sickness. The makeshift court that remained moved to St. James's Palace, for the rooms were less drafty.

Mary's health worsened and then, despite all precautions to keep the sickness at bay, she caught a terrible cold. Between the fever and the coughing, she barely spoke, and when she did, she always asked for her husband. Finally, her privy council came to her and asked her to make a final will and testament while she was still of sound mind.

Margaret stroked her hair as she turned away from them in her sick bed. Even now, after months of suffering, Mary wasn't ready to just give up. There was work for her to do. Work she did not trust Elizabeth to complete. After another bout of high fever that left her unconscious for two days, she could delay no longer.

She signed the paper and cried into Margaret's arms after the men had left. All her dignity vanishing.

"And n-now I am nothing but a d-dying woman," she said.

Margaret shook her head but could not bring herself to lie.

"I have signed my own death certificate. They are

now waiting like vultures for me to die," she continued between coughs.

Jane brought her a cup of hot ale and encouraged her to drink. It seemed to ease the pain in her throat, but she sent them away soon after, saying she wished to sleep now.

It went on like this for several more days. Mary would do little more than hear the mass in her room, sleep, and when she could, rail against her ill-luck. She continued weakening though — everyone could see it. She slept more and more and the spells of fever came on harder. No matter how many blankets and furs they piled on her, they couldn't stop her shivering.

Margaret was terrified for herself to catch this illness as well and couldn't help but hang back, not wishing to get too close to her dying cousin.

It was not peacefully that Mary passed from this world. Just as she struggled for much of her life, she struggled in her final moments as well. Many thought it was evidence of God's displeasure for bringing the inquisition and the Spanish to England and that it served her right. Margaret simply thought it was a cruel God that Mary served that had let her suffer so.

Dressed in a black gown that had been prepared for weeks now, Margaret was helped into the saddle by the Master of the Horse. In the palace, the priests were beginning to say the rites of the dead, but she would be riding to Hatfield with her husband. She did not have the luxury to mourn.

A great retinue of courtiers and ambassadors set off

with them, but it was Margaret and her husband that were at the forefront. They had the honor or privilege of dropping before Elizabeth's feet in deep bows.

"The Queen is dead. Long live the Queen," they said in unison.

# PART THREE

*What we resolve, only death shall dissolve*

*- Lennox Jewel*

# CHAPTER 9

## 1558-1559

THEY HAD TRIED to make it work. Margaret had tried to put aside her resentment and anger towards Elizabeth, and in turn, Elizabeth had tried to ignore her suspicion.

The first slight came when Margaret had not been selected to carry Elizabeth's train at her coronation. That honor went to the Duchess of Norfolk. So while Margaret rode closely behind Elizabeth, wearing her cornet for the magnificent occasion, she did not play an active role.

The second slight came when they were not given places at court. Of course, they kept their old rooms, but they were not given any titles or roles and thus, were left to feel like visitors. During an audience with Queen Elizabeth, they were given leave to return to Yorkshire. Effectively, they were being thrown out.

Margaret took this all in good spirits. By her distrust, Elizabeth was showing her how she feared her and saw her as a potential enemy. That gave Margaret power. For if she could make Elizabeth fear her, then she could influence events. Gather support.

In the north, she'd be around her own people and close to other Catholic allies, for Elizabeth had made it clear that she wished to make an Anglican church and leave the Roman one.

They took their time leaving for their home. Packing up the many goods given to them by Queen Mary and writing ahead to have Temple Newsham prepared for them.

The Queen had promised to be conciliatory to her Catholic subjects. She would not force them to convert as her sister had, but Margaret did not believe her. Queen Mary had promised the same, and it was not long until the fires at Smithfield were lit to burn those who did not obey her.

It was with this in mind that they did not stay long at Temple Newsham. It was their grandest home, to be sure, but it was poorly situated and land locked.

Margaret settled on Settrington to be their primary residence. Near the Yorkshire coast, the house was impressive and the nearby port made it easy to send letters to France and Scotland. Matthew teased her that she was preparing for war but she had not laughed.

"This is war. Or will soon be. Elizabeth is no true Queen," she said disrespectfully. "She had to bribe a Bishop to even place the crown on her head. The Archbishop wouldn't do it."

"Maggie..." He stopped her tirade with a warning but she shook her head.

"No, this is what she has brought upon herself. She is insupportable. How could she send us away from her? Well, husband, I will have you know that we have the support of the Spanish as well as many other Catholic lords. They do not like to see a heretic Queen on the throne..."

"Instead of who?" Matthew interrupted again. Looking at his dark expression Margaret knew he was serious.

"There are many heirs," she said, with an air of indifference.

"Wife, you are yet again heading towards treason. You shall take care not to slander the Queen. You cannot have pretensions to power now. We did not receive any. This is the very reason we were sent away. We might be entitled to a throne, Scottish or English, but we were not given any power with which to take it. We were excluded. It is safer for us to remain quietly here than to give Elizabeth any cause to have us accused of treason."

"You are wrong, husband. Now is when we fight. Not foolishly but we must press on with our claim. We have our sons to think about and their future. I refuse to be pushed aside and insulted. Also we are not alone, the Spanish Ambassador has written to me."

Matthew sighed heavily.

"That was very wrong of him to do so. Someone could have intercepted the letter."

"I did not know you had grown so fearful," Margaret said. She did not say it, but she wondered how she had become the brave one. She had always relied on her husband for strength and protection, but now he seemed fine to retire quietly out of sight.

"Do you have the energy to fight for this? What do you even hope to gain?"

Margaret wasn't even sure how to answer him. "I hope to gain my rightful place. To be given what I deserve as an heir to the Kingdom. As for energy, I will have energy until I take my last breath."

"Death. That is exactly where your ambitions will lead us to."

Margaret did not wish to fight anymore.

"Whether you wish to or not — until Elizabeth has an heir — we have a real stake in the throne. I won't miss a chance to take power if it is given to me. There are many who would support us."

"Maggie, this sounds as though you have already been plotting, and I pray to God it is not so. What support have you found?"

"Several, but if you must know, the earls of Northumberland and Westmorland are with us. The whole of the north is with us, I daresay."

Matthew looked as though he could not believe what he was hearing. She imagined that he wasn't sure if he should lock her away, report her to the Queen, or support her. So she took his hands in hers.

"Will you trust me?"

She could see him deliberating but finally he nodded.

"It will be on your shoulders — whether we succeed or fail," he said. "I want no part in it."

Even though he said that, of course he got pulled into

every little scheme and conversation she had. Perhaps he would have played court to Elizabeth and tried to gain her favor or even stayed quietly in the country where she wanted him, but Margaret had other plans.

---

For a while nothing happened. They did indeed live quietly, going about their daily routines.

Darnley had grown into a tall twelve-year-old, he was already charismatic and good at sports. Margaret was sure that this son of hers had the makings of a King. She made sure he would have the education of one as well. He did not apply himself the way she would have wanted. He enjoyed learning to ride and joust. He liked swordplay and practicing archery, but he did not sit down and debate with his tutors. He learned to repeat back his lessons to his tutors, but he did not absorb them.

He was young though, and Margaret was sure over time he would mature and become responsible.

If Mary of Scots did not survive or produce an heir, then there would be a really strong chance that Darnley might be able to press his claim to the Scottish throne. If somehow he was able to marry the Scots' Queen, then their union would unite claims to the English and Scottish thrones. They would be an unstoppable force. Even Elizabeth would quake in her boots.

But Mary Queen of Scots was married to the French Prince, and though he was not said to possess a good constitution, Margaret would not hold out hope.

With his strong claim in mind, Margaret spent time going over his genealogy with his tutor John Elder. She wanted it drawn up and set to paper. If he wondered what she would want with such a thing, he did not say but did as she bid.

The very paper now hidden away in her library could be seen as treasonous. It showed his strong claim to the Scottish throne. A claim stronger than even perhaps that of the Scottish Queen. To a suspicious Elizabeth, it would be enough to have them committed to the Tower, so for now, Margaret did nothing with it.

Then they received a visitor. He rode with a small retinue of men — the Spanish Ambassador Renard had come to pay his respects. Margaret saw immediately that among the party were some of Elizabeth's loyal adherents. It seemed he was not to be trusted to visit them alone.

"Welcome, my lord," she greeted him courteously. "My husband is out hunting with our son, but I am pleased to greet you and your companions. Though I was not expecting this visit."

"I apologize for that, Countess," he said, jumping down from his horse. "There was no time to write. I am being recalled by my master, but I wished to visit the English countryside before I departed and so I am taking a tour of this lovely country."

"And Queen Elizabeth could spare you?"

"Oh, I doubt she would wish me to be at court. Nor does she miss me, for her court is full of admirers and well-wishers."

"Well, come inside," she said, unsure of what to make of this.

They did not have a chance to speak alone until after dinner. He played his part well, touring the grounds and riding out to see the port town. That night he complimented his hosts graciously but seemed to be uninterested in speaking of anything but pleasantries. When Margaret offered to take him around her gardens herself, he refused.

That night, there was a light tap on her door and Matthew opened the door a crack. His loyal servant Nesbit came in, followed closely behind by a cloaked Renard.

Margaret would have giggled at his disguise, but this was a serious matter. She had a thick robe over top her nightshift and she hugged it tighter, suddenly feeling the chill of danger rush through her.

"Some wine?" Matthew offered him but the ambassador refused.

They took their seats around the fire while Nesbit stood by the door, listening for anyone outside.

"She has refused my King's offer of marriage even though it is the best match she could have hoped for. It seems she is intent on dragging this Kingdom back down the road to hell," he said, not bothering to mince his words.

"England has faced years of turmoil, but perhaps we can set it right," Margaret said.

Renard nodded solemnly. "My master has sought to bring this about for many years but we cannot give up so easily. Besides, the sainted Queen Mary had always doubted the legitimacy of this Elizabeth. Perhaps this will be all we would need to see her deposed."

Margaret's throat went dry at the thought and his dangerous words. She looked over to Nesbit whose expression had not changed. Still she would not be drawn into incriminating herself so easily. Her husband, too, shifted uneasily in his seat.

"All we wish is to ensure the true faith be maintained. Would the Pope excommunicate the Queen if she persists?"

"Yes, he was waiting to see who she would marry. There is hope that if she takes a Catholic husband, then he would ensure that England stays within the fold. But should she not... it would be imperative to make sure that the next person to sit on the throne is Catholic."

Margaret cracked a smile. "I doubt she will ever marry. She likes to flirt too much. She has no understanding of the importance of her throne and the duty she holds to it. She merely craves power. I hope you know that we would be willing to help the King of Spain as much as we can. We have always been good friends, I believe."

They talked nearly until dawn, but neither Margaret nor the Ambassador made any concrete promises. Their trust for each other was tentative and just as well, for Renard was leaving England, having failed in his mission to convince Elizabeth to take Philip as her husband.

It had become a habit to burn letters in the afternoon. There were a great many letters that seemed to find their way into her hands. Sometimes they appeared in her saddlebags, sometimes pressed into her hands by unknown servants wearing unmarked livery. Most spoke of undying loyalty, others had questions of what she would be doing. Most contained treason.

Her husband walked into her rooms in a flurry of energy. She nearly jumped, her heart beating faster at his sudden entry, but she continued feeding the papers to the fire.

"The Spanish Ambassador has been detained," he said without preamble.

She bit her lower lip but did not comment right away.

"We don't know why?" she said.

He shook his head.

"If he should talk about what we spoke about, we could be in trouble. We should think of fleeing."

"You would flee?" Margaret was surprised by his cowardice.

"The Queen is ruthless. I would not wait to see the way the wind blows."

"Fleeing would be disastrous. It would prove our guilt, and then we would lose everything we had. So no, we shall not flee," she said with such ferocity that Matthew looked aghast.

"We shall leave if I say so. Am I not the head of this household?"

She looked at him in such a way that he knew the answer.

"Dearest Mathieu, it is the age of Queens," she said, a smile spreading across her face.

Now she stepped forward, taking his hands that hung limply at his side.

"I love you. But I am done being afraid, and I shall never run again."

# CHAPTER 10

## 1560

IN THE END, it was not on them that the shadow of suspicion fell but on Katherine Grey, sister to Jane Grey. The Spanish Ambassador had not been content plotting with just them, it seemed. He cast a wide net to sow dissent in Elizabeth's England. Margaret could not be upset or feel betrayed. It was what she would have done as well.

It was William Cecil that wrote to her husband to inform him. In shame, the Ambassador sailed off for Scotland, but Katherine Grey had been questioned and kept under observation.

"He means to warn us to be careful," her husband warned.

"I know, but if they had wanted to pin something on us, they would have. It wouldn't even have to be real. I've seen evidence being fabricated out of thin air many times. Witnesses always ready to testify." There were countless examples she could have given him, but there was no point dwelling on the past.

---

The next foreigner to pay court to them was the French Ambassador. The tall wiry man made no pretense about why he had traveled to see them. He extended the friendship of the French King to them, looking to seek their support for Mary, Queen of Scots.

"She would be sure to reward her loyal cousins," he said. "The lands you are owed would be within her power to give to you in return for your service."

It was to Margaret that he spoke to, not Matthew who was doing his best to pretend he wasn't hearing this conversation. Pretending he hadn't been constantly disappointed by the French.

For her part Margaret wanted a better offer too.

She wasn't content pushing Darnley's claim to the throne aside in favor of the Scottish Queen, but what could she do? How could she play this to her advantage? She didn't think about it long — it couldn't hurt to foster love between them — two heirs united against Elizabeth would be better than one.

"The Queen is in a rage that they have declared Mary Queen of England," Margaret said. "She would not be pleased by your visit to us. You put us at great risk."

He gave her a terse smile. "You've been courting danger for many months. I believe our goals are the same, we do not wish a heretic to sit on the English throne. She has not married yet, but once she has a child, then you will be pushed further out of the line of succession. So any actions we take must occur before this."

"Elizabeth says she will not marry."

He laughed. "Of course, she would say that, but what woman can rule alone? She will marry. Her council keeps pressuring her to make a decision."

"I've watched my cousin hounded for years to change her mind and convert to the true faith but she clung on. I believe you underestimate her." She smiled then to placate him and she said, "But we shall be good friends to Queen Mary."

"I am pleased to hear that." He excused himself shortly after to rest.

Matthew turned to her. "What exactly do you mean by being good friends to that woman?"

"It means whatever it is I want it to mean. We cannot afford to make enemies of the French. I had hoped they might support us, but of course, they have a better candidate. Could you imagine through the Scots Queen they could get their hands on Scotland and England? My uncle feared this. France would become an unstoppable empire. Anyways, we shall play this to our advantage somehow. For now, we shall merely be friendly. I have promised nothing."

"You might have incurred Elizabeth's wrath over this nothing."

She shook her head. "We are making friends, and Elizabeth does not have the money or energy right now to deal with us. We have the support of many of the

Northern lords — the Percys, the Nevilles. Meanwhile, she has a bankrupt country, discontent from all these changes and poor harvests."

"This summer has been good so far, and please God, we might have a high yield on the crops so we don't fall into debt either. Perhaps your new friends would be happy to finance some of these projects of yours."

Margaret knew her husband did not like being pressed into a corner. She felt that as he aged, he wanted to do nothing but sit comfortably at his desk; away from the drama of court. She had to find a way to kindle the ambition that burned within him.

On his way back from London, the Earl of Westmorland Henry Neville stopped by. In his bag, he carried a letter for her from the French Ambassador.

"I was told to make sure it was delivered to you safely, and I did not wish merely to send it by any messenger. But there is another reason to visit. I hope you and your family will visit us this Christmas season if you are not called to court. Lord Darnley would surely benefit from the company of my own son, Charles, who's only a few years older."

Margaret nodded as she slid the letter in the sleeves of her gown to read later. With the practiced ease of a seasoned conspirator, she invited him and his retinue to stay for dinner.

"My husband is out hunting, but he shall be back

soon," she said. "I can show you our gardens. They've been newly planted and two pavilions built. There's a lovely view of the river from there."

He offered her his hand and they walked together, the members of their retinue following closely nearby. Philip and Charles were brought out by their tutor to greet this distinguished visitor and both showed their good breeding and training wonderfully.

When her husband appeared with Darnley, they escorted their guest inside where refreshments were waiting for them.

Everything was a calculated act to show their wealth and prestige. The Earl left impressed and promised that they would hear from him soon. This was so unlike Elizabeth's wild boisterous court. Their house was well ordered with a regular family structure and good Christian values. It was hardly surprising that the Catholic lords were flocking to them.

"What does the letter say?" her husband asked from the bed. His head was hurting after a long day, and he did not have the energy to read conspiracies.

"It is an invitation for Darnley to go to France, from the French Ambassador," she said, studying the flowing handwriting.

"For the coronation?"

She nodded. The sudden news of the French King's demise had shocked them all, but rather than ridding Queen Elizabeth of an enemy, it strengthened Queen Mary's claim.

"I think he should go. There is no reason he should not," Matthew said after a moment.

"It would be good for him to ingratiate himself with the potential future monarch. One that would be more sympathetic to us. He could even apply for the return of your lands to her in person."

She bit her nail, thinking but not daring to speak her thoughts out loud. Darnley was growing into a handsome man with all the accomplishments of a prince. If something were to happen to the new French King, Mary of Scots would be free to marry again, and why not unite her claims and that of her sons? The thought sent a shiver of excitement coursing through her.

But she couldn't even think of it as a possibility. It would be impossible. Improbable. She shouldn't even think of it.

"What do you think the Queen will make of it?" he asked.

She turned to him, her night robes swishing around her as she did so. "Oh, I expect she will be furious, but we have not been prevented from traveling. We are not part of her court nor could she really object to us sending Darnley to see her."

"She could see them as treasonous actions," he warned.

"There would be no proof. Aren't you friends with Cecil? Why not write to him to tell him that Darnley is going? After he has already left, of course. That way it will not appear as though we are hiding our actions, but it would also be too late for him to stop him from going."

"Maggie, you are turning into quite the plotter. Will you read to me? I cannot focus and my head is throbbing." He indicated to the letters on his bedside table.

---

It all came to nothing in the end. Darnley returned home from France with a purse full of gold and empty promises. Tragedy struck in Philip's sudden death. He had caught a fever that would not abate and died delirious after two days.

The weeks following had been hard. The family mourned heavily for many weeks.

Margaret tried her best to be optimistic. She focused all her attention on Darnley, dreaming of his marriage to the Queen of Scots. After all, he had met Queen Mary and spent plenty of time in her company. She was sure he would be remembered fondly.

Unfortunately, now they had to contend with Elizabeth's anger. Darnley had not been given permission to leave, and she was suspicious of Margaret's motives for sending him. She did not accept that he had merely gone to ask for his father's lands back. However, she did not have concrete proof with which to accuse them either.

Or at least, that's what Margaret assured herself of. She was still worried when her husband received a letter from his brother in Scotland.

"Mathieu, it would be foolhardy to involve yourself in this scheme. What would it achieve?"

"Your plans came to nothing," he accused but he also

apologized to let her know he hadn't meant it. "My brother is certain that Borthwick will turn the tide in Scotland, and then the Catholics will have a stronger foothold."

"How do you know this isn't a trap? Borthwick was sent by Elizabeth with a small army at his command to keep the country for the Protestants. He is her agent."

"My brother wouldn't be foolish enough to believe him if he wasn't sincere. After helping the Scots Queen gain control of the lords, she will be sure to know who to thank."

"I think it is risky. Even if he is not Elizabeth's spy, this plan of yours is likely to fail. There are too many unknowns," she said.

"What do you suggest then?"

She bit her lip as she thought long and hard. "There is always a chance this could succeed. Perhaps there is a way for us to play both sides. You should send that man of yours, Nesbit, to London to show these letters to Cecil but also to take this time to speak to the French Ambassador. That way Elizabeth can't accuse us of being disloyal."

"She might discover we have talked to the French. That won't look good either. We've been plotting a lot with foreign powers."

"Nothing has ever been proven." She brushed aside his concerns.

In the end, that is exactly what Matthew did. Nesbit met with Cecil in London, and they were rewarded with a letter thanking them for their loyalty.

It came as a shock to Margaret when news reached them through back channels that Nesbit had been arrested. He was supposed to have arrived the day before to report back but he had not arrived. Delays on the road were not uncommon, but to hear that he was now being held in the Tower for questioning put Margaret on edge.

"I shall have to go to London to answer their charges. If I come of my own freewill before a summons, they will be more likely to believe me," Matthew said.

"What did you tell Nesbit to say to the French? Can he be trusted?" She was pale though the day was warm and the sun shone brightly in the sky as they walked.

"It is better you did not know. But yes, I trust him. I only hope he burned any incriminating evidence."

"What would he have?"

Matthew frowned. "There's the genealogy that you had drawn up."

"I did not realize you sent that with him," she said, not able to keep the anxiety from her voice.

"What better way to convince the French ambassador to support our cause. We could be next in line for the Scottish throne."

"And has he written to you?"

Her husband nodded.

"You must show me the letter."

"I shall. While I'm in London, you must look after the children and not panic or do anything reckless. This isn't the time to be plotting. I would not doubt we are being watched."

Margaret nodded, she couldn't understand how

things had gone so wrong yet again. It seemed like all the enterprises of her life were doomed to failure.

When Matthew showed her the letter from the French Ambassador, making promises of help in gaining the Scottish throne should anything happen to the Queen of Scots in exchange for causing trouble in England, she slipped the letter into the pocket of her gown when he wasn't looking. He was so anxious about his trip to London that he had not noticed. Perhaps he trusted that she as his cautious wife would burn it.

But she would not do what he wanted. This would be her surety. Proof of a greater plot that might lead to Elizabeth forgiving them and show that she had not in fact been a party to the plot, but rather she was being used as a political tool.

If she played her part well, perhaps Elizabeth would even believe her.

---

Matthew departed, kissing their children and then her. He was in a merry mood, but Margaret could tell from the dark circles under his eyes that he had not slept well the night before. She watched him as he rode off with his retinue, holding Charles hand in one hand for comfort. Henry was too old for such a show of affection now so he opted for standing close to her.

"Will he be alright?"

It was uncharacteristic of him to show concern but it touched Margaret. He usually kept his feelings to himself, but behind his devil-may-care attitude, she knew he was a kind soul.

"Of course, there is no need to worry about him."

It was not long after he left that a royal courier escorted by an armed guard appeared on her doorstep.

"Her majesty wishes you to come with us to London."

"Why?" Margaret asked, not even bothering to pretend to be polite.

He gave her a rueful smile. "It was her command that you come. One way or another..." He trailed off at the implied threat.

"I cannot leave today. Nothing is prepared. She should have sent a warning."

He looked up at the sky as though imploring God for patience. "We need not leave for a few hours. That would be plenty of time for you to pack the belongings you need. Perhaps you will provide my men with some refreshment. We have had a hard ride."

Margaret found her mouth had gone quite dry, but she refused to show her fear. This was practically an arrest. She was being taken to London to be questioned and, surely afterwards, imprisonment in the Tower followed.

What could she do but comply? It would be all the worse for her if she made trouble and delayed. Yes, she had friends but they were not armed and ready to defend her. Nor was now the time to rise up against Queen Elizabeth.

She knew she was caught, but she did not yet know what Elizabeth wanted of her or what she even knew. She could survive this. She had survived worse than Elizabeth.

Darnley had wished to accompany her, but she expressly forbade it and left him in charge of his younger siblings.

In secret, she wrote to the Earl of Northumberland to do what he could for her and, if not, to look after her boys. The coded letter was sent by a trusted page.

There was nothing Elizabeth could call treasonous in the letter, and if she was questioned, Margaret could tell the truth that concern made her ask for help. She hated that she had to be so cautious and have an explanation ready for any of her actions.

---

Once in London, she was not given the chance to rest or even change out of her travel stained clothes. She was rushed through back passages into the privy chamber where she was finally allowed to sit while the members of the Queen's council appeared one by one.

Margaret caught the eye of Cecil who met her gaze with a kind one of his own.

"Get her majesty's guest a cup of ale," he said to a servant nearby.

A cup appeared in front of her, and she took it gladly, gulping it down.

"And when am I to see her majesty? I would like to thank her for her hospitality."

Her question was ignored by the men assembled, and she did not repeat herself though she was thoroughly angered by their rude treatment. This was likely all on Elizabeth's orders.

Finally, after they conferred quietly amongst themselves, Cecil straightened up and addressed her.

"Margaret, Countess of Lennox, you have been brought before this council to answer for your activities and plotting against the Queen's interests."

"I wish to see my husband," she said, ignoring him.

"I am afraid that is not possible."

"Why?"

"He is being held for questioning in the Tower. Perhaps your testimony today will shed light on the situation and you may visit him." He tempted her into confessing everything.

But she was not such a fool as to jump at the first carrot presented to her. Their questions seemed endless as the sun outside dimmed to a soft glow that indicated sunset was fast approaching.

They did not give her much time to answer them, but she was ready for this type of interrogation. They were trying to tire her out, confusing her before they trapped her into admitting her guilt. Unconsciously, her hand traveled to her pocket — her trump card lay within.

During a moment of reprieve she took her chance to speak.

"My lords, there has been a misunderstanding. If any mistake was made it was that we did not bring this to your attention sooner. I love the Queen as my dear cousin, and I would not plot to harm her. But I do know that there are many who would use my name to do so. They act without my permission and are simply troublemakers. The Queen knows what it is like when others plot in your name." She paused taking this time to pull out the letter from her pocket. "As you can see in this letter, it is not us who are plotting but rather the French." She had their full attention now.

A man ran forward to take it and Cecil opened the letter scanning it quickly. Margaret watched him carefully, only a slight frown betrayed his anxiety. He passed the letter around the table to the other men.

"How do we know you have not encouraged the French to put you on the Scottish throne? You may even have designs on the English?"

"Because we do not have any. If I could, I would lay my mind bare for you all to see my innocence in this matter. My husband and I are guilty of greed. We want his lands returned to him and our children to have the inheritance they deserve, but there is nothing else we desire. We have written to the Queen and this council many times on this subject, as you all well know."

"A pretty speech," Cecil said, though he wasn't looking at her but the letter that was in front of him again. "Very well, we shall deliberate on what you have said."

Margaret was brought to her old rooms at the palace, though guards were stationed outside the doors and she only had one maid to assist her. She did not care. She was sure had things gone differently, she would be on a barge this very moment heading for the Tower.

She prayed that night for the souls of her children and their safety.

———

She remained in her rooms for nearly a week. Tidbits of gossip were brought to her by her maid and Cecil, who visited once to get more details in regards to the French Ambassador. It seemed that now the council was focused on the French. They had bigger fish to fry besides her.

Margaret was not sorry to hear he had been arrested. It was his neck or hers, and the most punishment he would face would be to be shipped off to France.

As she gained more confidence that she would not be arrested or accused of anything, she demanded to see the Queen and speak to her in person. When that failed, she asked for a quill and parchment.

She wrote a letter to her husband, one to her chamberlain who was looking after her lands, and a lengthy one to Queen Elizabeth. Margaret was told they would be delivered, but she couldn't be sure they weren't tossed the minute they left the room.

Then she was allowed, after several inquiries to the council, to see her husband. He was brought to her rooms and they spoke for an hour. She was reassured he was in good spirits, though a bit shaken. He had been well treated despite the suddenness of his arrest.

The next day, he was allowed to join her permanently and they shared the last remaining days of their imprisonment together.

"We have been fools," he whispered to her as they laid down beside each other in bed.

"Hush. No, we haven't," she said curling up next to his familiar body.

"Shall we be home for Christmas?"

"I would bet you a hundred pounds."

"We could certainly use that money. So if you are holding out on me, I would like to know." His voice was trailing off as he fell asleep.

***

Margaret's predictions had been off the mark. They were released to return home before the end of November. During their stay, Margaret had not seen the Queen at all and it irked her to be thus ignored. If she was not to be a traitor, why couldn't she be a beloved cousin?

Still she counted her lucky stars and rode back to Yorkshire beside her husband, prepared to lie low for a season or two.

Her promise to herself to wait until the shadow of suspicion had passed them was broken when news reached them that King Francis II was dead, leaving Queen Mary a widow. Margaret waited with bated breath to see if some French prince would snap her up but none did, and it seemed like she was making plans to return to Scotland.

That Christmas she wrote letter after letter to her. First offering her condolences on the death of her husband, and then asking her to accept a miniature painted of Darnley. The implication was clear but she did not press the matter beyond her not so subtle hints.

Meanwhile the news from London was that Elizabeth was sick with anxiety. She began talking of marrying soon and looking at potential suitors more seriously again. She wrote to Matthew that she would be unable to help write to the Queen of Scots for the return of his lands because of this sensitive time.

Margaret was not fooled. Elizabeth would now never support their claim even if it meant they would have to leave England. She would rather keep them in prison than release them.

In February, after petitioning the Queen and all her councilors, Darnley was allowed to go to France in the retinue of the Earl of Bedford to offer Elizabeth's formal condolences and extend an arm of friendship.

Matthew laughed at what he now saw as her silly hopes, but she would not give up. Not now that Queen Mary was widowed so young and was still childless. If she did marry Darnley, then any child they had would be a legitimate prince and heir to the Scottish throne and even to the English one.

While Darnley was away in France, Margaret focused on Charles's upbringing. It was time he was found a tutor. Like Darnley, he was tall for his age with good solid features. His hair just as blonde, though he had lost the curls Darnley had. Unlike his brother, however, he was not as confident and seemed content to play quietly by himself rather than play with other children.

After interviewing a few candidates, she settled on Doctor John Ashby. He had studied at Cambridge before traveling to Italy to conclude his studies. Like her son, he was soft spoken, and she thought Charles might benefit from some gentle handling.

For once, she felt that the council had turned their focus away from her and her family.

It seemed that while the Queen was distracted with her, Katherine Grey, sister to the ill-fated Jane Grey, had gone behind the Queen's back and married.

This was a punishable offense. Already Katherine was seen as a contender for the English throne. Had not the Spanish Ambassador been plotting to whisk her away? Margaret shook her head at the foolishness of the girl. She had married for love to Edward Seymour, and now pregnant with her first child, was imprisoned in the Tower.

It was a scandal that she had married secretly. The only witness to this marriage was dead and the priest nowhere to be found. Margaret knew that Elizabeth would work hard to get the marriage declared unlawful and the child illegitimate.

If Katherine survived the Queen's wrath, she would

be shamed forever. Likely, this would suit Elizabeth who was always fearful of her heirs. She did not want competition for the love of the people.

After overseeing the planting of new crops on her lands and ensuring that the tenants concerns were heard either by herself or her husband, she set down to writing to Mary who was still in France.

Darnley's return had not been promising. The Queen of Scots was not ready to consider matrimony and seemed to want a greater marriage for herself. Though disappointed, Margaret could do nothing but continue her silent prayers that God would change her mind.

In August, it was known to everyone that Queen Mary was in talks with the Spanish to arrange an alliance. She was willing to marry Don Carlos, the son of King Philip, despite rumors he was insane. This also signaled her imminent departure from France.

Even if Margaret did not pay good money to stay abreast of the court gossip, she would have known this was likely to happen as it was clear from the nearby port that English ships were patrolling the channel. There would be only two reasons for them to do this.

Either they were in danger of attack or they were trying to catch someone. Margaret would have placed her money on the latter.

They were out riding, enjoying the sunny day. Margaret had arranged a picnic to be served to them. It was rare that she got moments like this with Matthew. Just the two of them. When they were newly married, they never had times like this.

As he poured wine into her goblet, she smiled at him, his beard speckled grey now. Her hands no longer smooth but starting to wrinkle despite the heavy application of cream. She was surprised to find that she still loved this man.

Her dreams of glory put aside as they listened to the sounds of nature around them. The horses grazing, birds twittering, the warm breeze sifting through the leaves. She was content.

"She has landed safely," he said, pulling her out of her reverie. "I thought you would like to know."

"Of course, I would. How is it that you know so soon?"

"I still pay many spies and not all of them are in England." He took a sip of wine.

Margaret took great pleasure in imagining how irked Elizabeth must be.

Lord Clinton, the Lord High Admiral, must be getting an earful from her. Maybe he would even lose his post on the privy council for this failure.

# CHAPTER 11

## 1561-1563

In November of that year Margaret was surprised to receive a summons to court.

"I believe she is showing me favor since that Katherine Grey gave birth to her son," she told Matthew.

"It would be nice to be at court — it's been too long and we have been entrenched here for many months," he said.

"I think you should stay here with the children. You weren't invited and I'd rather you were here in case..."

"In case what?"

"If she is displeased with me again, I would rather you be here to escape with the children." Margaret could not escape his questioning gaze, so she focused her attention on her letter.

"And where would we go without you? You know I could never leave you? Perhaps, if you simply stopped plotting, you wouldn't have to be thinking of all these contingency plans."

"Please, do not argue with me. I mean to keep us safe and our children."

"Then why do you try so hard for the throne?"

She did not have a response for him. It was a complicated answer — one that she fully did not know herself. But the desire for the crown to be given to Darnley, for herself to be declared legitimate, would solidify her value. She would no longer be merely the relative of a great person. She would become like her namesake, the matriarch of the Tudor dynasty, Margaret Beaufort. She would have founded a dynasty, and after she died, they would still remember her name. Perhaps it was all foolishness but desire ate away at her. She wanted this. She would see it happen.

---

Upon arriving at court Margaret was not able to see the Queen. She had taken to her bed, ill with swelling, and kept only those she trusted around her.

The gossip-mongers around court spread the news that she had become so bloated with bile and so swollen in size that none of her gowns fit. If rumors were to be believed, her hair had also fallen out and she had grown a second head.

Margaret did not pay much attention to them — she was familiar with her cousin's illness, and it was more likely that Elizabeth could not tolerate the discomfort nor being seen less than perfect.

Since she was here, she dined at the Queen's table,

happy to get fat at Elizabeth's expense. She waited in this uneasy state as Christmas approached. Courtiers trickled in with their invitations for the celebrations, and the ladies were all planning to put on a wonderful pageant.

She was surprised to find the Duke of Norfolk had arrived with his retinue — one that was greatly diminished from the one he usually traveled with.

When she asked him what the reason behind this was, he had said that the Master of the Queen's household had told him that the court could not accommodate so many people this Christmas season.

"She is a frugal Queen. You would think with two good harvests, her coffers would be able to handle the strain of a larger celebration but it is better this than debt," he said.

"Doesn't add anything to the grandeur of England — the Ambassadors are sure to report on the meanness of the celebrations. We will look weak in the eyes of Europe." Margaret couldn't stop herself from saying.

He nodded in agreement. His own lips pursed tightly as though the insult to England was his personally.

"Well, let us not dwell on what we cannot change," he said.

The court filled up and soon Margaret was pleased to find herself surrounded by her supporters. She wasn't such a fool to plot under the Queen's very nose, but she took advantage of the time to cultivate her relationships and gather news.

At length, she was told the Queen wished to see her and to be ready to present herself the next day after mass.

She attended Anglican services with a steely determination not to cause a fuss, but in the privacy of her rooms, she was given the holy communion as was a custom of the Catholics. Many friends came and attended with her, receiving the blessing of the Jesuit priest in her employment.

Dressed in one of her more demure black gowns trimmed with rich velvet, she entered Elizabeth's private rooms as elegantly as she could. Behind her a servant carried a chest containing a New Years gift for her cousin. A cape of gold brocade to be completed with a ruby pin.

She curtseyed three times to the Queen who was stretched out on a couch. She was working hard at keeping up an air of relaxation about her, but Margaret could tell right away that she was lying on the couch not for pleasure but out of pain. She was still recovering as evidenced from the lack of rings on her fingers — likely still too swollen from dropsy.

"Your majesty." Margaret leaned forward to kiss her outstretched hand in obeisance. The skin cool to the touch. "Thank you for your kind invitation this holiday season."

"Yes, yes," Elizabeth waved her hands impatiently, batting away the empty compliments that she must have heard a dozen times. "I hear you have been busy in Yorkshire."

"I have been maintaining my estates, if that is what you mean, your grace."

"Hmm. And what of all these letters going back and

forth between your house and Scotland. One might think you are trying to arrange a betrothal."

Margaret's fingers twitched but she tried her best to continue on as normal.

"I — my husband and I often write to the Queen of Scots to ask for the return of my husband's lands. It has been our greatest desire for many years."

"One might think that after so much failure you would redirect your efforts elsewhere. Though perhaps you already have..." As Elizabeth trailed off she pierced Margaret with one of her famous penetrating glares.

"If I have done something to displease you, please let me know how I can make amends," Margaret said without skipping a beat. She wasn't going to confess to anything. Besides it was not a crime to inquire about a potential betrothal for your child. It was only the actual act that was a considered treason. One she had broken twice in her lifetime already.

Elizabeth laughed heartily but it was a cold sound, containing no real mirth whatsoever.

"You may stop holding Catholic Masses in secret, for one thing," she said.

"Your majesty has not prohibited them, but I shall if you wish me too."

"It is not the Masses I object to so much but rather their subject matter. Do you deny that you plot and criticize me?"

"Of course I deny this. It is a falsehood but, if you would not believe me, then there is nothing for me to say. My family has always been loyal to the throne."

"Empty words and empty promises. What did you say to my council? That people are gossiping about you? That they are spreading lies? But if you lived such an innocent life, then I would not have cause to speak to you today."

"I did not realize I was brought to court to be interrogated. Again." Margaret could not hold the spite back from her voice. She wished now to be gone from this place. Why was she here, explaining herself to her younger cousin?

"You will be brought to court for whatever I wish. If I wish to summon you here to simply ask what you ate last week then I shall. "

Margaret did not flinch at the rage displayed by the younger woman. Even ill and sitting down as she was, Elizabeth could be imposing. Perhaps it was some power she had inherited from her mother, who could captivate a room and a King despite being a lowly commoner.

Robert Dudley whispered something in the Queen's ear and she laughed. Her hand reached up as though to grasp his but stopped.

"How old is your son now?"

"He is turning fourteen."

"A bit young for marriage, isn't he? Boys at that age belong in the school room or, better yet, serving as a page boy somewhere to learn his place in the world."

"He is being well taught," Margaret said, not liking where this conversation was heading.

"Yes, I am sure he is. But what subjects is he learning? Perhaps we can find him a place at my court."

"That would please him."

"I am sure it would not. I cannot abide an ungrateful courtier. So we shall strike a bargain. He shall not marry nor enter into any agreement to marry until I decide. Doesn't that seem fair?"

"Your grace, I do not understand."

"You shall cease to write your little letters to the Scots Queen. You shall not marry off your son, at least not for a few years until he has grown. You shall swear this to me now. I would not have it be said that I was unfair to you. That I did not warn you. So shall you swear?"

Margaret hesitated for the slightest of moments.

"I do so swear."

"You shall swear on your bible, and I shall have you sign a document."

"Whatever you wish."

Margaret retreated back to her rooms feeling defeated and guilty. She had been trapped into signing but there was little she could do. If she refused to sign, she would be defying her Queen. Now that she signed, she was giving Elizabeth a weapon to use against her. So if she was caught plotting yet again, there would be clear evidence that even she could not argue against. She could not plead ignorance.

It had been a mistake coming to court but again there was little she could have done.

Not much could be done about it.

"And when shall the painting be finished?"

"As soon as possible, I shall make it my first priority," Hans Eworth bowed respectfully. "It is not too late to change your mind. Linen is fine but for longevity I would recommend proper canvas."

"I appreciate your concern but linen will suit better," Margaret said, she looked over at her two boys.

Charles was shifting impatiently in his seat, but he did not speak out like his brother who had no shame about voicing his opinions.

"Mother, may we go now?" Darnley was pulling at his stiff collar. "This is dreadfully dull."

Margaret couldn't help being exasperated but nodded they could leave. She was doing this for them, but sometimes she felt like she was dragging them along down a path they would not have taken.

Shaking her head of such thoughts, she ventured from the room, leaving the painter to pack up his things. The paintings, once delivered, would be rolled up and sent in the dead of night to Scotland. A reminder to Queen Mary.

---

"Your husband has been sent to the Tower, and you are to come with me to London," Sir Hatton said coolly.

Margaret did not flinch. Were they to take up residence in the Tower permanently now? It might be more economical for Elizabeth to just gift them the place.

"And my sons?"

"They are to stay here. Sir Rossfair will look after them."

"They have done nothing wrong," Margaret said. "Why should they be placed under another's guardianship. They may come with me, or I shall send them to the Duke of Norfolk's household."

"Our orders are clear."

Margaret fought them every step of the way. She delayed as long as she could. Between taking a long time to pack to claiming she was ill. When they did finally depart, she left with the knowledge that Darnley would not stay behind to fall prey to Elizabeth.

They had planned this from before her husband's arrest. Darnley would flee to France as soon as he was able.

Thus, when a rider wearing the livery of Sir Hatton came riding up hard to meet them on the road to London, she knew what news he bore. Indeed, Sir Hatton gave her a scathing glare, though he did not dare say anything. Margaret knew with some satisfaction that Elizabeth would be furious they had let Darnley slip through their fingertips.

So she went with an easy heart into her old prison; the Charterhouse at Sheen.

Margaret had nothing to do but wait. The dullness was compounded by the fact that she was not allowed to go outside nor even open a window. Her ladies maids were sent away, and she was served by those loyal to Elizabeth. Everyone from the cook to the scullery maid was in her pay, ready to report anything Margaret said or did.

But after so many years, Margaret had learned patience. One way or another, her waiting would come to an end. It might not be the end she wished, so why the rush to the finish line? If this ended with her neck on the block, then she would savor these moments — these precious stolen breaths.

In her solitude, she prayed silently for the health of her children and the safety of her husband. Matthew was innocent of this plotting. She knew Elizabeth knew this as well, but she also knew that Elizabeth was not above hurting her to get what she wanted.

From her prison, she felt the weather shift from cold winter to warm spring. Occasionally, she received letters from her husband and Charles's tutor, but there was nothing in them except that they were alive and well for now. She was not told how long she was to remain at Sheen, only that she was never allowed to reply to the letters. She would have to wait. She knew this was Elizabeth's punishment.

When she was pulled before the Queen, she was given a new gown to wear. It was plain and the stiff collar itched at her throat, but she was happy to receive clean clothes — the ones she had been allowed to bring with her were worn and dirty.

She would remain resolute about not complaining about this mistreatment of her. If Elizabeth sought to humble her she would not let her succeed. She walked into the presence chamber with her head held high as though she was looking her very best and was not pale and smelling like a farmhouse.

Margaret waited with patience for the Queen to speak to her. She noted the many men seated in front of her as though this was a trial. Cecil held a stack of papers in front of him, and he wore a stern expression.

"Margaret, Countess of Lennox, you have been accused of conspiring against the crown, of witchcraft and of rudeness towards the Queen. You have been brought before this council to answer these charges," he said. His tone almost bored.

Margaret looked away from him and to Elizabeth, meeting her gaze full on. How dare she accuse her of witchcraft? She who was the daughter of an accused witch herself?

"Your grace, it does not matter what I say. I know in my heart that I am innocent of conspiring against you. I would never do anything against God or my conscience, for I am a God-fearing Christian woman. If perhaps I have not always shown you the great deference you deserve, then I do apologize." At this point she kneeled. She imagined Elizabeth rolling her eyes at her excessive show of deference but she didn't care. "I am loyal to you and the crown. I have upheld my promise to you. I do not know why I have been imprisoned, unable to see my children or my husband."

Some of the councilors gave each other looks. As a potential heir to the throne, mistreating her was not in their best interest. Nor would the world at large look kindly on a Queen who was so ruthless to her own kin.

Elizabeth remained silent after this speech. Margaret liked to think that she had stunned her but that might be wishful thinking.

"There are several witnesses that would come forth to report on your crimes. On top of this, we have letters written in your own hand and the horoscope of your son, cast with the purpose to see if he would inherit the crown."

Margaret could almost laugh. She had not expected this, besides did Elizabeth herself not have her charts drawn up by Doctor Dee? The horoscope they were accusing her of was drawn years ago for a son that had died in his first year. It seemed almost cruel of them to bring this up.

To acknowledge its existence would be a trap so she remained silent.

"I have no knowledge of such a horoscope. Since her majesty has come to the throne, I have not consulted with any astrologers, so if one was drawn for my son, it was not on my orders and they were very wrong to do so. Besides, I do not believe in the predictions of charlatans."

Cecil's lips pursed.

The questioning continued for what must have been several hours. Many she could not answer. How was she to know the conditions under which her parents married or what the papal documents said? When they questioned her why her father had not allowed her to inherit the Douglas lands, she knew that they were arguing a case for her illegitimacy.

There was nothing she could do to stop them.

They would twist information anyway they wanted, but as long as she could avoid the charge of treason, she would not care. She held an official document from the Pope himself declaring her legitimate. She did not recognize this court as having more power than him. Neither would any of the other Catholic Kings or Queens.

As the interview ended, she asked to be allowed to see her husband.

"We shall consider it," Elizabeth said from her throne.

Margaret bowed her head in thanks, and she was taken away again to wait.

This unending waiting would drive anyone else crazy, but she felt she had come out on top. By her calculation, she would be celebrating Easter in the north.

She was not allowed to see her husband but they were now allowed to exchange letters, and she was taken out to walk by the river every day if she wished.

Margaret relished these moments. Like a bird sensing freedom, she knew that soon she would be able to fly the coop. She was also aware that she would have to be careful lest she get herself into more trouble, so she did not plot or even speak out against the treatment dealt to her by the Queen. She took it all with level-headed coolness, making sure to show Elizabeth her gratitude.

Then in October, she received a visitor from Sir Nicholas Bacon, the Queen's Privy Seal. He inquired after her health and if she needed anything. As surprised as she was by this sudden attention paid to her, she remained stoic — asking only that she be allowed to see her husband and that he might speak to her majesty about being allowed to return home.

"I shall see if I can arrange for you to see your husband. And I shall make sure that more wood is brought up to your rooms. The weather is turning cold."

"You are most kind," Margaret said through gritted teeth. At home in Yorkshire, she could have large fires burning in every room if she wished and would not have to rely on charity. "How fares my cousin? I pray for her health and safety every day, but I have not heard from her."

She watched him carefully and did not miss the look of apprehension on his face.

"The Queen is well," he said simply, and from this, she knew that something was wrong.

"I am most happy to hear that. Would you be able to take her a message from me personally?"

"If I can."

"I merely want to inform her that I wish to serve her in whatever she wishes. I am hers to command. I wish to request an audience with her."

He looked skeptical at her words but did not dare contradict her.

"I will make sure she knows of your wishes," he said.

Margaret had a feeling that it would not matter. Perhaps the Queen was not in a fit state to even see her. Maybe she had caught the plague that swept through the country for as long as anyone could remember.

She had to find out what was going on, but how?

The next day Margaret eyed the scullery maid who came to clean the grate of her fireplace and take out the chamber pot. She fingered the gold pin in her hand. This was probably worth more than her wages for the whole year.

"You are a hard worker," Margaret said, not sure how to strike up conversation.

She looked up, surprised to hear herself being spoken to.

"I am not to speak to you, ma'am," she said just as briskly.

"Of course, my apologies. It's just it gets so lonely here day after day."

"You have fancy enough folk coming to visit you."

"Not often enough," Margaret said with a shrug, then turned back to her seat by the window, pretending to be disinterested.

It went on like this for a few days. Before finally Margaret spoke to her in her most piteous voice.

"I think I shall be stuck here forever. Sir Nicholas brought me nothing but false words of comfort. Why has the Queen not replied to me? Why am I forsworn?"

The maid spoke without realizing. "But she cannot reply to you." She immediately bit her finger to stop herself from speaking more.

Margaret rushed forward. "What do you mean she cannot reply?"

The maid took a step back. "I did not mean to say..."

"You must tell me." A pause. "If you know something, I must know. You see me here alone and praying every day for the Queen. I long to be by her side. I have little to give you for this small service but take this." She stretched out the gold hair pin. "Please, tell me."

The maid cast a glance around as though she was afraid someone might be watching, then reached forward to take the pin. "They say she is gravely ill. Not with the sweat. Something else. Everyone is nervous. I must go now."

Margaret sank back into her bed.

---

She picked at her dinner that night, a plain fish served with white sauce that reminded her it was Friday.

If Elizabeth died, then she might be freed. She might even be set upon the throne. She would abdicate for her son, though, as England needed a King or at least needed to feel secure with one on the throne. Never mind that queens could be just as efficient, if not more so, but it would be a good political move.

They wouldn't see her as a threat even though she was sure her son would listen to her. She envisioned herself as the power behind the throne.

This happy train of thought came to an abrupt end. Why would anyone place her on the throne? She was in prison. There were still other heirs that might come forth, no matter how small their claim.

She thought of Katherine Grey imprisoned in the Tower with her young son. She would be a potential candidate. With a Seymour husband at her back, they would surely rise to support her claim. There was the Queen of Scots, even the Duke of Norfolk could lay a claim.

Margaret could do nothing in her prison. She would be at their mercy, and they might think it would be expedient to have her secretly killed rather than to deal with another contender to the throne.

She looked down at the plate of cold fish, could this food have been poisoned?

Over the next few days, she fed most of the food she was given to the fire — eating only when she felt she might faint. She could not trust anything given to her but neither could she find the strength to starve herself.

It was the arrival of her husband quite suddenly into her rooms that both shocked her and brought her out of her wretched state of despair.

"Mathieu! What on earth are you doing here?" After she had leapt into his arms like she used to when they were newly married, she looked him up and down, making sure that he was well.

Besides being a bit haggard, he looked well.

"I have been released from the Tower and have been sent here to be kept under house arrest."

She grinned. "What a punishment. Soon you will be aching for your old rooms."

"And you are well? You look sickly," he said.

She blushed now. "I have been unable to eat well. All

I could think of is that they will poison my food. Perhaps I have been trapped here alone for too long. I should have taken the poison gladly rather than waste away."

"Nonsense." He pulled her close. "Anyways we are not to be killed in our beds. I have it on good authority that we shall be released from our prison soon. We have been thoroughly punished."

"I would say so."

"Don't be grim. You always knew that your games could end with us here. We have not suffered the worst consequence, so we should be grateful and thank God."

"What of Elizabeth?" She whispered this question so only he would hear. "I heard she was ill."

He nodded. "She was on death's door. But she survived the pox and God smiles on England. I am sure the council will be pushing her to marry within the year. She risked civil war by not acknowledging an heir. She was unconscious for most of her illness, so it would have been chaos."

"And Darnley? Have you some news of him?"

"I have written to him to prepare to return home to Temple Newsham, but not until he hears from either of us."

"Just in case?"

Matthew nodded. "Well, now that I am here, you may enjoy some more freedoms. I have sent for my books, and I have asked for a lute for you to play. Maybe some sewing? What would you like?"

"You expect to be kept here for a while longer then?" Her initial excitement faded.

"You can't rush these things. Cecil is working on our behalf. He believes there is a very good reason the Queen shall favor us."

"I suppose he did not tell you why?"

"No, but he had no reason to lie to me. You shall see. It will all come right."

It was November when they were released to come to court. Elizabeth was all friendliness and forgiveness. She scolded Margaret for her plotting, but then joked that she would have to employ her as her master spy.

The reason behind all this favor lay sleeping in a cradle in the Tower. Katherine Grey had been allowed to see her husband, and the result had been a second son born healthy and strong. Another claimant to Elizabeth's throne.

---

Margaret jumped as the seamstress fitting her accidentally poked her with a pin.

"Apologies, milady."

Margaret nodded, staring at herself in the full-length looking glass of Elizabeth's wardrobe. She had been allowed to have a royal gown tailored at the crown's expense. She wondered if Elizabeth thought this was enough compensation for months of imprisonment.

Still, the gown she had selected was a wonderful deep tan color, the underskirt would be cardinal red brocade. She was to wear it for the feast of Saint Paul's in two weeks and she intended to shine.

Her headdress would be refined, but she sent for her jewels from Temple Newsham to complete the image. She had grown older and definitely fatter than those early days in her youth. Looking at her hair dusted with grey, she was grateful for the French hood and cap that would cover it. There was nothing to be done about the deepening wrinkles.

Wasn't it just yesterday that she had been a desirable young woman that men were writing poetry to? At least she had grown wiser in these last years.

After she finished the wardrobe, she returned to her rooms to find Matthew there drafting a letter.

"Have you had news?" she asked.

"Darnley is sailing back to us as we speak. He shall be here within a day or two, if the weather is good. How was the fitting?"

"Good. But no dress can disguise how I have aged."

"Don't despair, be like our beautiful Queen. Ever confident. I have procured for you a present. Look on the bed."

Margaret went through the double doors to their private chamber inside. On the bed lay a small parcel wrapped in brown tissue. She opened this carefully. The package was incredibly light so it couldn't be a jewel. From the tissue fell two long white stockings, but she could tell immediately that these weren't just any ordinary stockings. She touched the material noting how cool to the touch it was. Italian silk! The edges were embroidered with little silver roses and lace. Extravagance indeed. These would not be itchy in the least.

"Where ever did you get these?" she asked, peeping around the corner to see a grinning Matthew smiling up at her.

"I bribed the Master of the Wardrobe to find out where the Queen orders hers from. Only the very best for my wife."

"You do spoil me. I've never seen such fine silk before."

"Some new technique. Much finer than our English silk."

Margaret dared not ask how much it would cost for all her stockings to be as fine as these.

---

The banquet was lavish, though Margaret knew for a fact that the Queen had been stingy with the meat. She was ever careful with her expenses and hated to spend when she didn't have to.

Margaret could see her always at her desk in the evening, looking over the ledgers like some miserly moneylender. It was not very grand of her. Perhaps the commoner blood that ran through her veins made her unable to see that such matters were beneath her.

She had held her tongue, of course, and not said anything to her nor gossiped about it behind her back when Lady Sydney had tried to drag her into trouble one night as they drank wine by the fire.

Elizabeth's schedule was punishing. She woke early and went riding well into the afternoon before pausing to break her fast. She heard mass then attended to state business. After dinner she would enjoy some entertainment with her courtiers. Most times this meant card games.

She had teased Margaret when she had won a hand.

"See, Cousin Margaret, I have won the pot, though whatever you have is mine anyways."

Margaret did not rise to her bait.

"As always, you are the victor." She raised her glass in toast to her. She found on nights she was forced to attend these gatherings that she tended to drink a lot more than usual.

The next day, when Margaret was late arriving for the hunt, Elizabeth forbade her from joining them.

"If you are unwell, then perhaps you should stay behind and see a doctor."

"Your majesty, I would be ready in just a moment. I could ride to catch up to you — there is no need to wait for me."

Elizabeth laughed. "We have not waited for you. I wait for no one." She glanced at Robert Dudley.

Margaret swallowed hard and looked at the courtiers around the Queen, finding her husband looking crestfallen.

"I shall do as your majesty commands and return to my bed." Margaret curtseyed as politely as she could. It was hard work keeping the anger from showing on her features.

She must appear serene. She must appear grateful — even in the face of all these incivilities.

Elizabeth seemed keen to reward them after the humiliation she doled out to them. Like her father before her, she liked to use the rod then offer sweets. Margaret and her husband were summoned to the Star Chamber and invited to sit.

Elizabeth was all friendly smiles. "I have drafted a letter to send to Scotland. It entreats the Queen to deal kindly with you. I hope she shall do as I bid her and return your lands to you."

Matthew's mouth hung open. "Your majesty is most kind to trouble yourself over this."

"Her highness is very generous," Margaret supplemented, hoping her husband would gather himself up.

"It is, indeed, generous of me. So I hope that this will show you that it was not in bad faith that I made you swear to me that Darnley shall not marry the Scots Queen. I reward those who serve me well."

"I shall always serve you to the best of my abilities," Matthew said.

Margaret looked down to the floor to hide her annoyed expression. He did not need to sell himself so cheaply. How were they to know that this letter would even be sent? But she dared not say anything.

Time would tell.

# CHAPTER 12

## 1564

It seemed that Cecil had spoken to Elizabeth, and she decided to be kinder to Margaret. She was informed that she would be allowed to draw material from the royal wardrobe to have a new gown made for her for the feast of Saint Swithin.

It was a step.

More importantly, Darnley was invited to join the celebrations, and Cecil had assured her that he was sure to be favored by the Queen.

---

The family reunion was held in their private rooms with no one to interrupt Margaret from hugging and kissing her boy. Nor could his protests stop her from fussing over him and pressing him to eat more.

"Mother, I am a grown man."

"You shall always be my child. I have been worried about you alone in Scotland."

"I was hardly alone, John Elder was with me, and I had my loyal companions too."

"Who?"

"Sir Henry Talbot and Thomas Scott." He was rolling his eyes as he spoke.

Those were his hired retainers. Margaret could roll her eyes too and see how he liked it, but she was glad to see that he was fine. If anything, he had grown more mature in the time he was away.

"Where did you send your horses?"

"My hunter went lame in France, so I traveled here on a borrowed horse. You shall have to buy me another."

She was too tired to argue over the expense with him.

Afterwards, they brought him before the Queen, and he delighted her with his pretty manners and fair speech.

"You have a very pretty child, Countess," Elizabeth said in one sentence both complimenting and insulting him.

"He is nearly twenty, your majesty," she said by way of contradicting her.

"He is clean shaven and his curls remind me of a babe's," she said in return.

To stop them from discussing his appearance and its merits, Darnley stepped forward.

"I am overcome by the opportunity to be in your majesty's presence. Your beauty has no competition, nor have I seen such a striking show of royalty."

"Ah, you have the makings of a poet. Maybe even a politician."

With a grin, Darnley doffed his cap and jumped into a verse.

"Loving in truth, and willing in verse, my love to show."

She applauded him for he was indeed talented.

"I hope we shall see you at court more often," the Queen said.

"Thank you so much, your grace."

Margaret was happy to hear this and for the Queen to be acknowledging him. Everyone could see he was well brought up and indeed a strong heir.

They retreated from her presence joining the throng of courtiers as Elizabeth stepped down from her throne. She partnered Robert Dudley in a galliard. The musicians seemed to play an endless stream of songs for one dance after another.

Margaret encouraged Darnley to join the dancers and watched him as he danced with one pretty girl after another. They all seemed to be charmed by him, for indeed he was good looking.

However, she hoped he remembered that she had told him that he was not to become overly flirtatious. Elizabeth did not approve of such behavior, especially when it was directed at one of her ladies and not to herself. Margaret knew her to be a vain woman, but she supposed she had also been when she had some looks to boast of. Now that they were gone, she was content to no longer compete.

Surprising news came to them by a royal messenger bearing the insignia not of their Queen Elizabeth but of the Queen of Scots. In a sealed crate, he brought with him the letters patent for the Lennox lands in Scotland.

The parliament had voted on the matter, and upon receiving pressure from both Matthew's brother and the Queen herself, they agreed that the attainder against her husband should be lifted, and he should be gifted the lands that should be rightfully his.

Matthew was in shock and Margaret thought the happiness might kill him.

"Sit down, you look like you are about to faint."

She ignored the scathing look he gave her.

"You know what this will mean for us, don't you?"

"Besides more money and influence?"

He chuckled at that. "Well, in the broad scheme of things, yes, it will. But it will also mean we will be separated. I shall have to travel to Scotland."

"I can come with you. Why should I not?"

"I doubt the Queen will give you permission. We are under suspicion."

"Was she not the one who wrote to Queen Mary herself?"

"I am sure she has come to regret it. She is changeable. What will we do if we are to be separated?"

"Are you asking me if we should flee to Scotland and turn our coats?" she joked.

"It's an option but a highly unfavorable one.

"We would lose all our English lands. And..."

"I would never consider giving it up, you should know that by now."

Margaret visibly relaxed, her shoulders were no longer tense. "Fine but I wanted to argue with you a bit longer."

"Do you think that the Queen means to separate us? If she will not allow me to go with you, and she conceives some reason to keep you in Scotland..."

"That is the worst case scenario. I would not be separated from my dear wife that long. I promise you, we shall be together. I did not realize that, after so many years, you would miss sharing my bed and that you would be willing to run away to be with me."

"I am happy to see, after so many years, you have not lost your sense of humor. I would miss you deeply. For how much of our married life have we been kept apart?"

"You have a liking for plotting, so I'm surprised we are still together now," he said.

"The old argument. How often have I heard you say that?"

It was not long before Matthew departed for Scotland. Margaret traveled as far north as she dared, taking Darnley with her. He had been displeased to be taken away from court, but Margaret thought it would be prudent for him to say goodbye to his father.

"You shall have to help manage the lands while he is

gone. It is high time you take responsibility for your own upkeep. You are forever gambling and ruining horses. There is not an endless supply of money, you know."

"Mother, you can be so infuriating. Father never speaks to me like this," he said.

But she did not let him play her. This was an old game of his, trying to turn the tables on them to convince them to fight amongst each other. They usually fell for this, and he was never properly punished. Thus, he had gotten away with stealing from the dairy and going out carousing with his young friends — returning home late and so drunk that he had been sick all over the venetian carpets.

They said a sorrowful farewell to Matthew. Margaret had not meant to appear so solemn as though he was going off to war. But for whatever reason, it felt like this was the beginning of the end. A growing feeling in the pit of her stomach that this might be the last time she saw her husband. They were to live apart for at least a year, and she knew what a year could do. Had not many of her children been born, learned to walk, and then perished within the span of a year?

She would pray daily for their reunion.

"Write to me often," she said.

He gave her one last kiss before leaping onto his horse. His movements altogether more energetic and youthful.

"God bless you, Mathieu," she called after him, unable to stop her voice from cracking.

"Mother, you are making a scene."

She could slap her son but she restrained herself. Then thought that perhaps it was true. It was not dignified of her to show such emotion.

"Let's return, we have a long ride back if we are to go all the way back to Yorkshire."

"Shall we not visit the Duke of Norfolk on the way?"

"No, I don't think the Queen would approve."

"Must you write to her to tell her everything we do."

"If I have to. We are being watched; it is better to be transparent, and I know she wouldn't like it if I did anything that seemed to be gathering support. I am to be a country lady and nothing more."

"You have royal blood flowing through your veins."

"Hush." She patted his arms.

---

The days felt empty and quiet, even though Margaret was always busy working with her secretary and meeting with everyone from merchants to farmers to sort out their lands in England.

Money from the crown was unreliable, and she wanted Charles to receive a proper inheritance. She didn't want him to be beholden to anyone. It was only a pity that this realization had dawned on her so late in life. If only she had taken the issue more seriously earlier.

She wondered often what Matthew was doing in Scotland. Was he thinking of her as often as she was thinking of him? During the day, she missed his steadying presence that always seemed to soothe her. At night, she missed his warmth and the way he would inevitably wrap his arms around her in a tight embrace.

The truth was that he was probably too busy to miss her. He had risen to being a man of great importance — one with many enemies. She wasn't sure how he would fend them off. How long it would take before they would be reunited?

A man dressed in a fine velvet suit appeared on her doorstep. He was a handsome young man she recognized as one of the men who visited with the master jeweler.

He bowed low to her and introduced himself as Roger Kurt.

"I bring the jewel you ordered." He motioned for a man standing behind him to bring forth a small wooden chest. "It is the finest I have seen come out of our shop." At these words, a small blush had spread over his cheeks. He clearly wasn't used to bragging.

Margaret smiled. "I cannot wait to see what he has sent me. Are you to stay and dine here for the night? Do you have other business or will you ride for Scotland immediately?"

"I shall be happy to rest here, but I shall go on to Scotland if that is what you command," he said.

"You may go as soon as you are able, and you may carry my letter to my husband to accompany this gift."

"Shall you open the chest, milady?"

She looked at him curiously. He seemed excited about its contents. "Why are you so eager for me to do so?"

His cheeks reddened. "I helped my master draw up the plans for it."

Carefully, she opened the lid.

Inside, sitting on a piece of blue velvet, was a large golden locket. Even after this quick glance, Margaret knew it was very fine and intricate, that there was more to it than met the eye.

Two figures held up a crown decorated with rubies and an emerald. Gently, she lifted the blue heart to reveal the accompanying words of death shall dissolve. She imagined him wearing this jewel as a proud memento of their love. She put it back in its case.

Her heart swelled with the thought of her husband receiving this little gift from her. She had worked endlessly with the goldsmith to come out with the perfect design. He would know how precious this was.

"Very beautiful," she complimented the man.

---

That Christmas was merry despite Matthew not being there. Margaret hired musicians and a troupe of mummers to perform for the large crowd of visitors. They invited everyone from their lowest tenants to their landed retainers to dine with them and partake in the celebrations.

Margaret handed out little gifts to her staff. Her maids in waiting received some of her old gowns that they would use to transform into beautiful new modern ones.

She spent most evenings recounting the day's events

in letters to her husband. In the morning, by the bright sunlight, she would read the letters he sent her.

News was good.

Though the manors and castles on his lands had fallen into disrepair, the farms had been well tended. He hoped to be able to send back a heavy purse of gold to her after the harvest. They had long decided to keep their treasury in England as their primary holding, as Scotland was still tumultuous.

The political scene was rife with strife. The Queen kept trying to press her Catholic religion on her people, who had become more Protestant than the English. She was now at odds with her brother, and her councilors were pressuring her to wed.

Word was that the negotiations with Spain had failed.

King Philip's son was a madman and hardly suitable as a King Consort. Mary seemed unable to bring herself to marry a man outside her religion, so she could not accept the suit of the Earl of Aaran, who actually had also been Queen Elizabeth's one time suitor.

The Earl, who had acted as regent for Scotland, was finding it hard to give way to a woman, especially one with such outdated views of her own country. Queen Mary had left Scotland as an infant and returned a French woman in all but lineage. Her behavior was altogether foreign.

She had grown used to ruling with an iron fist in France. For there the monarch had absolute power. Things were different in Scotland, and family politics were the order of the day. The monarch ruled by the will of the people, nothing more. But instead of working with the lords of her realm, she was fighting with them. She was not listening to what her people wanted, she thought she knew best.

All this Matthew wrote to her in subtle wording. For all her faults, Elizabeth ruled her people well, and despite the faction fighting, there was not the civil unrest present north of the border.

# CHAPTER 13

## 1565-1567

In January, she received a letter that said Darnley should come to join his father in Scotland. Her husband claimed that he needed assistance with managing his lands, and that, as his heir, Darnley had much to learn about the governing of these lands. The letter ended with a request that Darnley bring with him a few items he ordered from merchants in London.

Margaret rode south to speak with the Queen in person and see her son. Darnley was with Elizabeth, a part of the large group of young men that entertained her and joined in all her games and excursions.

"Why should I let your son go to Scotland? What business could he possibly have there? Look at him. He is still but a child. His father can spare him."

Margaret smiled, weary of the games. "I am sure your majesty is right, but it is my duty to ask you..."

"You would love for him to go. Perhaps you would

love for him to write pretty poetry to another Queen," Elizabeth interrupted.

"We have sworn that we would not press any suit on his behalf without your permission. I would not dare. It is my husband that asks for him to join."

"Come, speak candidly with me. I shall not be disappointed if you are honest with me," Elizabeth said, a kind smile pasted on her face.

"I do hope he will make a splendid marriage, but I would hope it is one that has your approval and is beneficial for him. I would not wish him to be so far from me, so you need not worry yourself over that. But he is your subject, and you will order him as you please. I only make this request of you at the behest of my husband."

"Cecil, how many letters have left the Countess's house for Scotland?"

"Many, your grace."

"But how many were to my husband?" Margaret said, fuming.

"Most of them," Cecil was forced to admit.

"Your majesty, there is nothing wrong with communicating with one's own husband."

"Lady Margaret, you are not under questioning. I shall consider it. I shall speak with the Scottish Ambassador. Summon him to see me, Cecil."

"As you wish, your majesty."

It was several days before Margaret received her reply.

"You are allowed to go," she said, the jubilee in her voice was unmistakable.

"Where am I to go?" Darnley looked up from his game of cards.

"To your father, of course. I am sure he shall present you at court as well. It is only proper that you should."

"Mother, did you lie to the Queen?" he said, his voice low and conspiratorial.

Even here, alone with her son, she would not admit her private hopes to him.

"I did not lie to the Queen. You shall go to help your father."

"And I did not see Master Scott leave in the dead of night yesterday?"

"What?" She did not say more. "Why were you awake to see him go? Where were you?"

"I went out," he said with a shrug.

"I see. What were you doing, besides gambling away your inheritance? You must try to curb your impulses. It is not becoming of one of your rank."

"Mother, you do not know what is fashionable nowadays. Perhaps in your youth it was how you did things, but if one is to appear lordly one must not worry about such thing as money. Gambling is merely entertainment. It would not do to count every penny."

"You are lucky you were born the son of a lord and not that of a farmer," Margaret said wryly.

"I would rather die than be a farmer. But my destiny belongs in greater things than worrying about sheep and the state of the crops."

"Son, those are still important to you. They pay for your lifestyle. You should be concerned with them. In years of trouble, they are what will keep your people fed. It is your responsibility to look after your people."

"I know that," he said.

But Margaret wasn't sure he truly understood. Then again, he was young, she told herself. He would learn.

He was at that tender age where he wanted to impress his friends. Besides, he lived at a competitive court. The Queen distracted her courtiers with trying to gain her favor rather than actually doing something productive. It was less about policy and more about who rode the best, who could compose the best sonnet.

What did these young noblemen know of war? They were too young to have remembered the skirmishes into France or even the ones into Scotland. They heard tales and songs and craved to show their bravery on the battlefield, but since no chance of that came, they were intent on competing in the arena of sport, music and dance.

Matthew assured her that in good time her son would learn that these empty pursuits were not rewarding. He would learn true governance through life experience.

He had been trained since he was young for this.

It had been drilled into him how to be a nobleman. How to manage his estates and how to manage his finances. He had learned to read Latin and spoke French with great fluency. He was a well rounded boy, but he chose to put these accomplishments aside unless there was someone to impress. If there was no one around that he had not won over to his side, then he was content to be lazy. He had gathered an impressive number of friends around him.

She thought he had earned it, for the most part. This lovely son of hers. His golden curls and sharp features that reminded her of a royal prince. She envisioned such a future for him that she would trust in God to show him the way. Especially since now he was getting way out of her reach or control.

---

He departed for Scotland with a small retinue to not alert Elizabeth to his having any alternate plans. Margaret wrote to the Queen often about the preparations for his departure, that she was anticipating his return, and how happy she was that the Queen had given him this chance.

Privately, she knew that Robert Dudley's suit for the Queen of Scots' hand had been denied. Even though he had been made Earl of Leicester, she had been insulted that Elizabeth would even offer him to her.

Now more than ever, it seemed that Queen Mary would be keen on marrying Darnley. They were both older and wiser. And he was the best candidate, as other Catholics had fallen through. There seemed to be a shortage of suitable candidates, and people were not clambering to ally themselves to Scotland. She was not tempting enough.

The opportunity was perfect for Darnley.

---

She opened the first letter from Matthew with her heart pounding. She could not wait to read it. In fact, she was so excited that she could barely read the words on the page.

Taking slow breaths, she calmed enough to focus on the words.

> *My darling Maggie,*
>
> *Henry has arrived in good health and he seems to be making himself at home here. He makes friends easily but of course a man with a loose purse is often able to draw many people to him. But he carries himself well. I brought him to be introduced to Queen Mary and she seemed impressed with his learning. They danced together and everyone commented on how well suited they seemed for each other.*
>
> *I have matters to see to here. And I have to make peace with Douglas. I hope you are in equally good health and spirits.*
>
> *Give my blessing to Charles and remind him to not make excuses to avoid his lessons.*
>
> *Love,*
>
> *Matthew*

Margaret read and reread the letter. It seemed so banal. But she was struck by the comment that the Queen had deigned to dance with her son. It gave her fuel to hope. The spark that she had held close to her heart suddenly engulfed her like a flame. After so many failures, perhaps this was the moment. This time would be different.

---

News from Scotland slowed. Her husband kept his letters devoid of any suggestions or hopes he might have. Margaret knew this was not because of anything other than caution. People were stopping by her house to give her news that Darnley seemed greatly favored by the Queen of Scots. Everyone was keen to say she preferred him above all others.

It made Margaret think of Robert Dudley and Queen Elizabeth. However, she hoped that, unlike Robert Dudley, her son would have greater prospects, but still she dared not hope. Dared not write anything. She was conspicuous in not writing anything to Queen Mary. All her letters were to Queen Elizabeth and Cecil.

Still, all her caution was for nothing.

For Elizabeth was just as paranoid as her father before her. Though perhaps this time she was not fearful without reason.

Margaret knew that when she saw the dust being kicked up on the road that this was not good news. She was expecting no visitors, so these must be men coming up from London, from the Queen.

She had not received news from her husband in two weeks, which was unusual. She sent for the chamberlain and steward and began shouting instructions at them.

First, they were to delay these visitors as much as

possible. Then they were to pack her things — in light trunks and make sure jewels and gold were ready for her departure. Charles was to be sent with his tutor to the Earl of Westmorland under the guise of an apprenticeship. They were to go now.

They might have an hour to do as she wished. She had told them what to do in her absence and that her husband would send orders if she was unable to do so. She was also to receive regular payments from her coffers.

"Where do you expect to go milady?"

"To London — where I do not know. But you must swear to me on the Holy Mother of God that you will do as I wish. Promise me?"

"I do. I swear, I shall see your lands managed in your absence."

"Good. You shall be rewarded for your loyal service."

"God Bless you, your ladyship."

The men had come from the Queen with a warrant for her arrest. This time there was no pretense. She was not to be invited to court to be questioned. She was being sent to her old haunt, the Tower. She knew this as surely as she knew that the Pope was God's representative on Earth.

She was given little time to pack, but since her servants had a head start, she was able to bring a decent trousseau with her.

Heavy capes and fur lined gowns would keep her warm in the Tower. Her finery was left behind and her simpler dresses were brought. She hid a purse of gold among her underthings hoping she would be allowed to keep this.

They were happy that she was ready so quickly and had not protested. She did not bring to their attention that the Queen had overlooked what was to be done with her youngest son. He would be safer in anonymous seclusion. Let him be forgotten instead of being dragged into the Tower with her. Let him remain in the school room learning his lessons, rather than counting the days in the Tower.

A footman helped her into the saddle of her own horse for the ride to London. Though she suffered bouts of ill health, she was not so unwell that she had to go in a litter and she did not wish to appear as though she was being dragged.

Her jailor was displeased by the people lining the road to shout out blessings on her. They saw this as the persecution of an innocent woman. Margaret had been a good landlady to them. Generous with her alms and always taking up works in maintenance of the roads and lands.

Their loyalty was not to a distant Queen they never saw but to the one that handed them out bread and coins after Mass on Sunday.

Margaret did not make a big show, but she smiled and looked from left to right as she passed. Her jailor would not have reason to complain about her.

The journey did not take as long as she felt it should have taken. Before long, she was consigned to the Tower. At least she was not subjected to the long road any more.

The weather was hot and she was allowed to stop as often as she would have liked. Any more and she would have been unable to stay upright in the saddle.

Her trunks were searched but she was allowed to keep the purse of gold. She was glad for the clothes she brought, for the nights were drafty and she knew that she might be trapped in here well into winter. She tried not to dwell on the fact that, like Katherine Grey, she could be imprisoned here until her death.

It was not long before she knew why she had been imprisoned. Queen Mary had shown her son more than just favor. First she had named him Earl of Ross and there were plans to elevate him even further. From the beginning, there was talk of the two of them marrying, but it was not until recently that the deed was done. She had married him. She had not even wanted to wait for a dispensation from the Pope.

So this was why Margaret was now locked away.

Had she not promised that he would not marry the Scots Queen? She had even promised he would not marry at all without the Queen's express permission.

It did not matter to the Queen that she had sent no instructions, nor had she conspired directly this time. Of course, she had hoped but that could not be illegal.

She had always pressed the claim of her son to the Scots lords, so of course they would know why he was a good suitor for the Queen. Besides her son had a way with women. They were attracted by his charm and easy manner. How could it be her fault that the Queen of Scots had fallen in love with him?

When she was questioned about this, of course she confirmed that this was love. Why else would the Scottish Queen demean herself by going to her son's sickbed to tend to him herself? At the risk of endangering her own life? Or so the rumors told her.

But this seemed to make no difference. She would remain confined to these four walls. Once a day, she was taken for a stroll along the parapets of the wall. Precious moments she cherished.

She was not given paper and pen with which to send messages to her husband. She bribed the maids with the coins for the precious tools of communication and then bribed them again to send the messages to her husband. She had no way of knowing if he received any of the strips of thin scrawled writing to try to conserve the paper she bought at such high prices.

It was autumn before she found a folded piece of paper beneath her pillow when she laid down to sleep.

"Keep safe. You are mother of a King. Hopefully a grandmother as well. God be praised."

She had not heard. Elizabeth must have forbidden this news to pass to her. She did not even know when her son had been married to the Queen of Scots. It was ironic that the greatest hope of her life had taken place and she did not know the details. She did not know if he had been crowned yet or what the people thought of him.

Weeks passed before anymore news arrived.

He had not been crowned by the Queen who, like Elizabeth, was not willing to share power with her husband. Margaret's husband had bribed the guards to send her another purse of gold.

She was sure this was a quarter of the amount he intended for her but she was grateful. With winter fast approaching, she would need to pay for more wood to keep her rooms warm. Elizabeth would be pleased if she caught some illness and perished here, but Margaret was happy to thwart her plans.

The days ticked by again.

Slowly, the excitement of the news left, and she was alone once again with only her desire for more news. The next piece of news she received was from her husband. He said he was writing from his home in Scotland on the borders. Why was he not at court? She read on.

It seemed things were going sour between her son and his wife the Queen. He had been trying to throw his weight around but without much avail. He was seen as foolish and with no actual intellect to help govern a Kingdom.

"Lies," Margaret hissed, unable to stop the words escaping her lips.

The good news was that the Queen was great with child. Margaret did the sign of the cross and kissed the letter. Her grandchild. She would be a grandmother to a future King. She was sure it would be a boy. She was so sure. Perhaps after the birth of Mary's child, she would have to capitulate and crown Darnley as she should have done from the beginning.

Either way, this child was a blessing and Margaret knew she would pray day and night for his safe arrival.

She was not sure what to make of the other news that her husband was ousted from court and that her son was disregarded by the Scottish nobility. It's true that if they valued fighting and strength then her son, though not lacking in that area, was definitely softer than most.

He had not seen war. He had merely fought in mock tournaments. His strengths lay in other areas like poetry and hunting. But he was definitely accomplished.

She would pray that whatever rift was caused between him and wife would be healed.

Despite her concerns, she could not forget how glad she was that this had happened for her family. Because of this marriage, they were now part of the royal family of Scotland — and of England.

She had to survive to see her husband again, to see her son and that future grandchild that had still not been born.

She wrote two letters that night. One to her son, telling him of her plight and to congratulate him on the pregnancy. The other was to her husband to tell her more about what was going on.

Elizabeth was still furious with her. She was furious with her councilors for letting Darnley go to Scotland. She was furious that now such a threat lay north of the border. They were sure to be pressing for her to marry and produce an heir herself.

Margaret, who had been so sure before that she would indeed marry, found she had changed her mind. Elizabeth could never bring herself to marry. That would mean giving up power, and on top of that, the business of giving birth was terrifying to her. It was a woman's duty to suffer to give birth to the future but Elizabeth was a coward. Margaret knew she would never bring herself to carry a child in her own belly. But all the better for herself.

Her son and his child now had a better claim to the throne than ever before.

There was no point questioning her as she was by now ignorant of all events. The constable of the Tower visited occasionally, and his wife came to sit with her and gossiped about the latest fashions and events but it was never the news she wanted.

Finally she heard the news that she had been waiting for. The Queen of Scotland had given birth to a live healthy boy. She celebrated her son's victory, and though she was sad that she could not be there to hold him and smell that fresh baby scent, she was happy in her heart that she had lived to hear of his arrival.

He would be called James after the Queen's father. In what seemed to Margaret a cruel twist of fate, Mary had asked Elizabeth to stand as Godmother at his Christening. Perhaps she was doing it to encourage her to name him her heir officially. Margaret could not know for she had still not heard from her son.

Her husband wrote little except to send her more gold and that he was writing daily for her release.

Margaret had gotten used to the Tower after all these

long months. If Elizabeth was going to have her killed, she would have done so by now. No, she was likely doomed to wallow here, but she would not do so in self-pity.

When the Constable's wife arrived with freshly baked sweet buns, they celebrated in her rooms.

"I am a grandmother now, you cannot imagine how happy that makes me," Margaret said, taking a large bite.

"It is indeed momentous to hear such news. You must be very proud indeed," she replied.

"And the Queen? Shall she travel to Scotland for the Christening?"

"No, but she is sending a proxy, and they said she is giving him a cradle made of gold."

Margaret smiled. He deserved nothing less. But perhaps she should also free his grandmother.

"May I write to the council? I cannot help but asking if I would be allowed to attend his Christening."

"I shall bring you some paper, for it would be cruel not to let you ask. But my husband shall have to read it before you send it," she said.

"Very well." Her spirits somewhat dampened.

---

The reply had been no. She expected nothing less but she could sleep easier knowing that she had tried her best. Often she found herself daydreaming of finding a way to escape. She would go on the run and make her way to Scotland. Her daughter-in-law would protect her from this Queen of England, and in return, she would support her to take down Elizabeth.

She often fantasized about riding into England at the head of a large army. How Elizabeth would quake then!

Her husband's letter carried as much detail as he could cram in the small letter about Prince James's Christening. He tried to describe everything from the robes that were draped around him to the font in which he was immersed.

Darnley and his wife were still fighting, he said, but perhaps the days to come would soften them to each other.

Margaret frowned at this. There was no excuse now. Darnley deserved his rightful place by the Queen's side. He would find a way to bring her to an understanding. After all, how would it look to their son to see his father so demoted?

# CHAPTER 14

## 1567-1568

THE MONTHS DRUDGED on in this manner. Matthew's letters were not as frequent, for he knew that he had no good news to report to her.

Then one morning as she was working on some sewing, a knock came at her door. It was unexpected and jolted her out of her silent thought. Her heart began hammering in her chest as a small troop of guards came in. Cecil in the middle of this throng, his face drawn.

This was it. Elizabeth must have decided to have her brought to trial. She waited.

"Countess of Lennox, I hope you are well. I do not know if you have heard anything from Scotland. But I come to you now with grave news. But perhaps you may have heard already?"

Margaret wasn't expecting that. How many times had these words been spoken to her? From the sad pitying looks on their faces, she thought that her grandson was dead. As so many babes die young in their crib. She found her throat was dry.

"I have had no news for many weeks now," she said, admitting her ignorance. She needed him to say it now and quickly. She wanted this done.

"It is your son, Lord Darnley. I fear he has been assassinated."

"Lady Margaret, can you hear me?"

Margaret felt herself blink as though she was another person. Her body ached and she let out a groan as she tried to shift.

She saw the court physician standing above her, the constable's wife beside him. A bit further back was Cecil.

"Wh-what h-happened?" she said, a hand going to her head which throbbed.

"You fainted and fell to the floor. We could not revive you for about an hour," the woman said.

"Is it true? Is my darling boy dead?" She looked at the people around her, wildly going back and forth between one and the other.

"I am afraid it is so," Cecil spoke again.

Margaret felt her vision darken again but this time she fought it. She shook her head and asked for some water.

"How could this be? Who could have done such a cruel thing? He was innocent. What..."

"Lady Margaret you must rest now. I shall return tomorrow and answer all your questions. You must rest," Cecil said.

The physician nodded.

So they had discussed this. They would tell her the most awful news, and then let her stew in unknowing for as long as it suited them.

"Sir, I have done nothing but wait all these long months. I shall find no rest if I do not know what has happened."

The two men looked at each other.

"Very well, but if you look as though you are about to faint, I shall cease to speak until you are well. Your son was living apart from his wife the Queen of Scots, and in the night there was an explosion. He was found dead outside. We still can't be sure what happened, but he was not killed by the explosion. There were marks on his neck that indicated he was strangled."

Margaret felt herself go still. She wanted to collapse in a fit of rage and sadness, but there would be time for that later; for now she wanted to know. "G-go on."

Seeing she had collected herself, he continued. "His servant was murdered as well. A knife through the chest. We have operatives in Scotland now working to discover who committed this crime. We do not know more."

"And my grandson? And the Queen? What of her?"

"Your grandson is safe, God bless him. Queen Mary had visited her husband the night before, but she had gone to a party and was not at the residence when the accident took place."

"And do you truly believe it was an accident? You call it that but I doubt it was from what you tell me. How can he have been accidentally s-strangled." She choked on the words.

"I misspoke. But officially that is what it is being called."

Margaret let out of a sob that was a half laugh. "It was that traitorous bitch. I know it was. She was fighting with my son. She wasn't going to crown him, and then she decided she would rather have him out of the way. I just know it!"

"I cannot comment," Cecil said. "I do not have any more news to bring you, but Queen Elizabeth sends her deepest regrets and promises to not rest until the matter is fully investigated."

"That is very kind of her indeed."

"And you are to be allowed to leave the Tower and have your son, Charles, to mourn and take care of your affairs," he added.

"Very kind..." Margaret was trailing off. She could not think of her anger towards Queen Elizabeth at the moment, or the fact that, if it wasn't for her, perhaps she would have been in Scotland. Perhaps she could have mended things between the couple or prevented this tragedy.

"What of his body? Where shall he be buried?" She suddenly rounded back on Cecil.

"I expect in Scotland."

"But... he should be buried at Temple Newsham. In the family priory. That country was no home to him. I can't believe she would be allowed to have a say in what happens to him after what she has done to him. His last moments were probably fighting with her."

"I shall tell your worries to the Queen, perhaps we can negotiate something."

"Thank you," she said, turning back to the window. It was all she could do to keep from bursting into tears. How had she not known this tragedy had occurred? As his mother, she should have felt something when it happened.

------

She was at Somerset Place within the week. She was dressed in deepest black and the Queen's tailors were hard at work making her more dresses suitable for mourning. She found Charles pale faced and dressed in black himself.

"I heard from Father," he said, his eyes watering.

"We shall talk later, son," she said, stepping out of the litter. She was too weary to talk to him now.

"May I help you with anything?"

Margaret looked at him. He was always so eager to please. This younger son was now all that was left to her. He had none of the impertinence Philip had. Nor the confidence possessed by Henry, but perhaps, unlike them, he would survive. He would be their future.

"That is very kind of you to ask. Has there been any letters for me from your father? Does he know I have been set free?"

"I wrote to tell him three days ago, but there has been no news yet. Do you think he will come home? I do not know what I am to do?"

She patted his shoulders. This young child had been burdened with the worries of a much older man. He had never been raised to be the heir, and he had been cast suddenly into that role with no mother or father to guide him.

"I shall rest and then I shall summon you to my privy chamber. You may ask me anything you wish."

He nodded.

She found she could not sleep though, in her long nights in the Tower, she had yearned for this time. To be in her own bed. The soft feather mattress beneath her, the freshly laundered sheets.

She pushed off the blankets, letting the cool air hit her. If she could not rest then she would be productive. She went to her writing desk and penned a long letter to her husband. She wanted to know more. She wanted to know what would be done.

Her tears stained the letter, in places the ink ran but she wrote onwards.

The despair was settling into the deepest anger. She had seen her son through all his childhood illnesses, he had lived through so much and now he would be taken away not by some act of God but by the work of a spiteful woman.

And her innocent grandson? What would become of him?

After she was finished, salting the letter before sealing it, she summoned Charles.

She regarded him differently now. Her last precious child. He would have to be married as soon as he was of age. She could see how precarious the situation was. He would have to be protected from everything — illness, ill intent. She would never let him leave her side.

---

Her husband returned but it was in shame. He was fleeing for his life yet again. Matters in Scotland had turned sour, and his unpopularity marked him out as a dead man. There was turmoil. The Queen had remarried.

"What do you mean she has remarried? My son has not yet been dead a month!"

He had tried to wrap his arms around her to stop her screaming, but she merely pushed him away.

"Who?"

"Bothwell. I was so close to convincing Mary to arrest him for Darnley's murder. Some say he kidnapped her. Others say that they had been lovers since before this."

"Are you saying they plotted to kill Darnley together?"

"She may have had a hand in it. We can never truly know. The Queen is not investigating the matter further. She said an accident killed her husband."

"Our son! Is he to be left unavenged? I shall march

into Scotland and tie a noose around her own neck, and then we shall see if it is called an accident."

"She may have had nothing to do with it. You cannot accuse her like this." Matthew was all good reason but his face was drawn and pale. Like her, he looked like he had lost a lot of weight and had not been sleeping well.

"I can accuse her. I know it was her. Or that she ordered it. You said it yourself that they were fighting. Perhaps she wanted to put him aside."

"She wanted to petition the Pope for a divorce."

She gasped at his admitting this piece of news.

"Are you certain?"

"I am but I am also certain that the night before he was killed that they had made up. They were to be friends."

"She probably told him that to put him off his guard. A devilish trick no doubt," she said, biting her finger. "Bothwell was always her man. She only pretended to let you investigate the charges to keep you off the scent. You must tell me what happened. From the beginning."

"Very well but let's have some food. You look like you are ready to collapse," he said.

"As do you," she said and sent for the food.

They talked all night. After the assassination, Mary had called for an investigation. She was scared and horrified by what had happened, but at the same time she seemed to be unable to act.

"I was in charge of the commission, and I found enough evidence to bring certain men to trial. Bothwell included but the Queen ignored my letters and pleas. I was at a loss for what to do. Perhaps she feared his power, for he had gathered a lot of lords to his side. He has money and charm and a good amount of ruthlessness on his side as well. Our faction was small in comparison and the Queen's inability to act rendered them all the more powerful."

"You talk as though she did not collude with them."

Margaret watched him as he stroked his beard. "I would like to think the best of her. I cannot understand why she acted the way she did. She was in shock, perhaps. She is definitely not as strong of a woman as are you or our Queen Elizabeth. Ever since they assassinated Ritzio in front of her against her very command, she has been fearful. This is a kindness I am doing for her. Otherwise, I like many others would think that she had a hand in her husband's death. The death of our son and the father of her child. I believe she is a good Christian woman who would not do this. I cannot see how she could bring herself to plot such treachery."

"Can you not?" She was scowling now and she couldn't help it. She was almost furious with him. How dare he speak such kind words about Mary and try to invoke pity for her?

He probably saw her expression change, for he was quick to continue.

"Of course, if evidence comes forward, I would believe it most heartily. But you did not serve at her court. She was a good woman for all her faults."

"All of Christendom calls her a whore and a murderess, but yet you persist in calling her good?"

"Madge, please let us not fight about this. I am in no position to fight. I have ridden hard to get to safety, and I do not wish to hear angry words from you. Let us rest and we shall talk tomorrow."

"I have had no rest since I heard the news," she bit her finger to stop fresh tears from springing forth. "I cannot sleep and, as the sun rises, I think to myself how can I be alive when my precious Henry will never see the sun again?"

"Hush, he has found peace in heaven." Matthew was now stroking her head.

"I cannot rest until his murderers have been brought to justice," she whispered. "I swear, I shall not rest."

———

She was true to her word. She could not close her eyes until, out of sheer exhaustion, she passed out. She woke and saw that still the sun had not risen. She must have only slept two hours at most.

At her side, her husband was sleeping deeply. He was indeed looking exhausted after his long travail. She could see how thin he had become, and was it her imagination or was his beard sparser of late?

She looked away from the sad sight. They were growing old and their own list of successors was growing thin.

They traveled to Windsor as soon as possible. They would speak to Elizabeth the moment they were admitted to her presence.

The news from Scotland was bad. The Scots Queen was overthrown by her brother Moray's faction.

They wanted to see justice be done.

It was not only Cecil but Robert Dudley and Throckmorton who spoke words of consolation to them. They promised to help support them. After all, they too wanted justice done and they were more than happy to encourage Queen Elizabeth to not let the murder of one of her kin to go unpunished.

Margaret also knew that Cecil was more than happy to discredit Queen Mary. Up until this point, she had appeared to be the most likely of candidates for the English throne should Elizabeth die, but how could they stomach such a notorious woman now? Not only had she plotted to murder her husband, but now, mere weeks after his death, she was married to another.

Elizabeth too was kind to them.

"I am sorry to hear of your troubles, dearest cousin," she said. "I have spoken to the treasury to release some funds to you so you may have something to live off of."

"We are happy to hear of it, for it is true our financial situation at the moment is dire." Matthew was just as nice in his replies to her. He spoke as if it was not the Queen that had confiscated their goods and lands.

It was left to Margaret to press for more.

"Please your majesty, and what is to be done about the murderers of my son? My husband was thrown out of Scotland for trying to bring them to justice. This cannot be borne."

"And I swear to you it shall not be." Elizabeth was

passionate. "I have written to Moray that he must continue to work for the inquiry to continue. I have also written to Mary to demand she put aside Bothwell and bring Darnley's murderers to justice, but as you know, she is not in a position to do so."

"And what of our grandson?" Margaret asked. "We fear for his safety. My husband says he is in danger of being pulled apart in faction fighting. The Hamiltons are trying to get their hands on him, and then they may even have him killed, as they claim they have a right to the Scottish throne."

"This is well known. We are concerned for young Prince James as well. He is my Godson. I have written to the council to release James to us."

"You have?" Margaret couldn't help but interrupt.

"I have indeed. I think it would be prudent to have young James raised here in England, under the safe guardianship of his relatives where no stain would taint his honor."

"You believe Mary is guilty as well then? She knew of the assassination of my son?"

"Nothing is proven." Elizabeth looked over to Cecil who nodded. "But it does not look good."

---

Elizabeth provided them with an extended lease of Somerset Palace and the loan from the treasury was to be paid out shortly. Soon they would be able to travel north and put everything to right. But they were heavily in debt now, especially since they had no revenue coming in from Scotland.

It was there that they received an unexpected visitor.

Her half-brother, the Bishop of Moray, was on their doorstep. Clearly, he had ridden hard.

The edge of his coat was coated with mud and his expression frozen in grim horror as he jumped down from his horse.

"Shall we go inside to talk or do you wish to rest?" Margaret asked, ignoring any social niceties.

"Yes, but let me have a glass of ale. My throat is dry."

She led him inside. Matthew, who had been resting in bed, had joined them too.

He took two swigs of the warm ale and sighed. "You must speak to Queen Elizabeth. There is far more brewing in Scotland than the feuding that has been going on for generations."

"What do you mean? Can you speak more bluntly?" Margaret said, looking to her husband whose brows were furrowed at his words.

"They may have her executed. The Scots lords are finished with Catholics and they are finished with the Queen. They thought she might die of her miscarriage and would have been happy. Now they are itching to have her out of the picture entirely. She managed to raise a force of six thousand men, but they were defeated over a week ago now. She has shown them that she will not sit back quietly while they take control."

"That is her problem, she would deserve nothing

less," Margaret said. "At least then one of Darnley's murderers would get what they deserve."

"Margaret, what will happen to James? If she is killed. What if they call him illegitimate?"

Margaret rounded on her half-brother. "Could this happen?"

"I do not know. But I need the English Queen to help us. We shall have nothing but war and strife in our Kingdom and what then?"

"You want her to influence who will win?"

He nodded. "If she uses her power to keep things together, then the country won't fall into utter chaos. They are fearful of an English invasion. We have not the men nor strength to repel such an attack."

"She hates war, she would never ride into war for Mary. She despises her too."

"They are Queens of the same bloodline. If one Queen can be deposed so can another," he said with a shrug. "Tell that to your Queen."

"She is sure to know it already. She fears that her own people would see her pushed off the throne. They love her but she always fears losing that love."

"As she should. She is a clever woman." He took another deep drink from his ale. "I bring letters with me from Moray and the English Ambassador. Will you take me to court to meet with the Queen? It is to be an unofficial meeting. By all accounts, I have come here to give you news of your lands and grandson."

"We shall. How is James?" Margaret asked.

"He is being kept safe at Stirling for now. Moray is a

good guardian. He loves his nephew but I am afraid that many will try to gain control of the King."

"The King? Is that what you called him?"

He nodded looking abashed. "I am afraid they shall force the Queen to abdicate in favor of her son. I wouldn't be surprised if, by the end of summer, he is crowned in her place. So you see he will become a pawn in the hands of stronger men."

"By all rights, you should be the regent," Margaret said, turning to Matthew who went visibly pale at her words.

"Madge, you cannot be serious. I have just fled for my life. What of my lands?"

"They were shared among Moray's men. I am afraid it will be hard to regain them," George said.

"You see, I have nothing. Once again we live off charity." Matthew sunk back into his chair.

"We shall speak to the Queen. Who else could she prefer? She won't let Moray be regent. For once, I think I am correct."

"Why wouldn't she? He's Protestant and friendly with the English."

"She won't like how it looks. He betrayed his own sister and deposed his Queen. He has set a dangerous precedent and shown that he cannot be trusted. Maybe she won't move against him now, but she won't like seeing him in power. Mark my words."

By the beginning of August, news had spread all over England that Queen Mary had been forced to abdicate. She was practically on her death bed when the men who had once professed to be her loyal adherents pushed their way into her private chambers and made her sign. Threatening to have her killed if she refused.

So of course, she signed. She had seen her own secretary dragged from her room and stabbed. She knew exactly what these men were capable of.

It seemed, though, that Elizabeth had managed to save her. She had put great pressure on Moray and the Scottish lords not to harm Mary or else they would face England's retribution.

As expected, Moray was elected Regent of Scotland

Margaret and Matthew were often traveling to meet with the Queen or Leicester to hear the news from Scotland and to petition the Queen to demand James be brought to England to be raised by them.

"Matthew, I think we should commission a painting for King James."

"Margaret, we are just finally beginning to refill our coffers. I hardly think now is the time to go around commissioning portraits."

Margaret looked at her husband, weak from another attack of a cold. He was on the mend, but his illness just threw everything into sharp relief. They were getting old. Already she was older than when her own mother had died. At fifty-three, she felt she had lived more than one lifetime. She could not be sure if she would ever have the chance to meet James in person. Their many attempts had failed. Who then would remind him of his noble father? Who would remind him to seek justice for his death? It was she that wore the jeweled locket she had commissioned for Matthew over her heart. A constant reminder of their love but also the sacrifices they had made and would continue to make for their loved ones.

She explained this to Matthew as plainly as she could. "I think it would be the most important legacy I leave behind. A surety that if I cannot live to see justice be done, then someone else will after I am gone."

"You have become morbid in your later years."

"I have become a realist. I cannot sit idly by. Already I feel powerless."

"Very well, if you think it is important."

"I will rest easier."

The grim painting was sketched out in autumn. It was fitting that the day was just as dreary as the portrait was to be.

Margaret had met with the painters, often discussing what she wished to see. Her fingers touched the rough sketch as though she wished it to tell the future. "Arise, Lord, and avenge..."

She loved the words. She knew them by heart. They were her private prayer every night before she went to bed. She hoped one day that James would say these very words aloud.

The painting was delivered to them after the new year and, though Matthew continued to complain about its cost, he was too late to stop it.

Their money troubles continued.

Though they were now back in their own home at Temple Newsham, things were very different. Even a lot of their furnishings had disappeared. Government officials had sold off some of the more valuable pieces while Margaret was imprisoned in the Tower. The mismanagement of the crops and the animals meant there was little money to restore the house to its former glory. They found it hard enough keeping the rooms warm in the winter.

Margaret wrote often to the Queen complaining about the mismanagement of her agents and how she was sure that the Queen would rectify the issue by giving them a larger loan.

Predictably, the tight fisted Elizabeth was not forthcoming with the money. She promised to help but said her own finances made it impossible for her to do more.

That spring, Margaret took to her bed with a fever. She feared she would not wake up but, as her fever abated, the pain in her stomach began. She felt as though the anger and misery she felt at all the mishaps in her life were becoming too much to bear. At night she dreamt of little baby Henry, the first of her children to perish. She dreamt of Maggie cooing over Philip. She dreamt of Darnley's reprimanding face. The thought she had failed him terrorized her.

Only Mary's death would satisfy these demons. Only

Bothwell hanged for murder would soothe her inner turmoil.

Matthew summoned doctor after doctor to her bedside, but she believed it was her own resolve that finally pushed her to her feet.

How could she let herself waste away when she should be finding ways to avenge her son?

# CHAPTER 15

## 1568-1570

GOD HAD HEARD HER PRAYERS. Mary had run to England in search of sanctuary.

She seemed to have managed to escape her captors and traveled to England under disguise. The news had spread throughout the Kingdom like wildfire. Margaret and Matthew had not hesitated to pack up their things and head to court immediately.

Now they might have justice. The exiled Scottish Queen was under Elizabeth's control.

"Do you think she will actually act?" Margaret asked him. "Shall we place a wager on it?"

"Queen Elizabeth has promised to bring her cousin to account for her actions. I have faith in her. At the very least, I know she would not dare place Mary back on her throne."

Margaret thought otherwise but what good would it do her to voice her doubts now? It was true though. All of Europe was scandalized by Mary's behavior, Elizabeth was at liberty to act as she wished with her treacherous cousin, and Margaret wished to encourage her to do so.

They arrived at court to find their Queen quite agitated by events. She was torn by how to proceed. On one hand, she should show support for a fellow Queen; on the other, she should throw Mary into a dungeon.

As always, she seemed to have settled on a middle ground.

Mary would be placed under house arrest — unofficially. For as long as it took to clear her name of the accusations of murder and adultery made against her.

"Your majesty, you must know of her guilt. There can be no doubt. Should she not be in the Tower?" Margaret pressed, working hard to keep the irritation out of her voice.

"It is a complicated matter, Lady Margaret," Elizabeth said. Her eyes darting away from her to Leicester standing nearby.

"Her majesty is doing all she can. The matter is delicate but she has sworn to find justice for your son, and I have even promised to work on this. Will you not trust us?" he said.

Margaret swallowed her protests.

"I did not mean to imply that I did not trust your majesty. Of course, you will do what is best for the realm. I am merely a mother in deep mourning. I am also concerned for the welfare of my grandson left alone in Scotland. You must forgive my impertinence."

"That I can easily grant you," Elizabeth said, a small smile on her lips. "Please know that this affects us deeply. I shall keep you abreast of any developments."

"Thank you." Margaret gave a deep curtsey.

It took weeks before they gave up the chase. It was clear that Elizabeth had imprisoned her cousin but, at the same time, had no real intention of pursuing the matter further.

"Would that she would die in prison," Margaret swore aloud.

Matthew checked her. "It is not very Christian of you. I am sure Mary does not enjoy being kept away from her country under close guard."

"That is hardly a punishment. I heard that she dines under a canopy of estate. There are even rumors that Elizabeth is trying to restore Mary to her throne. What if this is true?"

"It cannot be." Matthew shook his head. "She would be a fool if she did this. The situation is merely precarious at the moment."

"Fine."

"Margaret, please be sensible."

She did not listen to his pleas but left the room. She would go write a heated letter to her cousin to outline the very good reasons why Mary should remain in prison and be brought to trial for Darnley's murder.

"You will be happy to hear Bothwell has been imprisoned," Matthew began.

"Where?" Margaret gasped unable to have any patience.

"He was captured in Denmark by his would-be friend King Fredrick, as it so happens, and he seems unable to buy his freedom. Queen Elizabeth is pressing that he should remain behind bars as well."

"God be praised. I shall pray now only to live long enough to hear of his death," Margaret said.

"I knew you'd be happy to hear this news. Shall you sleep easier now?"

Margaret nodded. Her prayers were being answered slowly but surely. Then she could rest.

The ache in her bones served as a constant reminder of her mortality. She must find a way to convince the Queen not to restore Mary to her throne.

They had lived in a constant state of unease in regards to Mary for nearly a year. But it seemed that Mary had not been idle in her imprisonment either. Despite the heavy guard placed on her, she was somehow able to coordinate a rebellion on her behalf.

Margaret and her husband were at Oxford with the Queen when the news broke that the earls of Northumberland and Westmorland were openly raising their tenants alongside the Duke of Norfolk. They planned to free Mary of Scots from her prison and place her on Elizabeth's throne.

Elizabeth had no army and her treasury was empty.

Everyone was walking around on edge. No one had the desire to see a Catholic set up in the place of their Protestant Queen. Especially not such a notorious one.

Despite having nothing to do with these plans, Margaret was still treated with great suspicion. It was true that these were her old conspirators, but she would not support Mary's rise to power. She wanted to see her head on a spike decorating traitor's gate, not with the English crown on her head.

It was a miracle that saved Elizabeth. The rebellion was squashed.

She had mustered up a decent sized army and the local people supported her wholeheartedly.

The rebel army had been given misleading reports overestimating the size of Elizabeth's army and they quickly lost heart. The Earl of Sussex had come to her aid, mustering an army to march against the lords. Parliament also added their support behind Elizabeth and voted to pay her an additional payment that let her arm more men to send north under the command of Baron Clinton.

The Duke of Norfolk, who had doubted this plan from the beginning, had taken to his sick bed instead of taking to the field. Now Elizabeth's wrath would rain down on the northerners and even him, her own cousin. Within the month, the Duke found himself convalescing in the Tower rather than his warm rooms.

Margaret couldn't help but feel a grim satisfaction that Mary had failed. Now, surely, Elizabeth would punish her. Mary had signed her own death warrant by her plotting.

Disappointingly, Elizabeth was slow to act, but she no longer upheld any pretense of wishing to find a way to restore Mary to the Scottish throne. This Margaret counted as a victory.

The earls had managed to escape Elizabeth's wrath. One fled abroad and the other to Scotland where word was that he was imprisoned by James Douglas. Margaret hoped they would eventually face the consequences for their actions, but she was content that they were marked men for life.

———

Margaret and her husband returned to spend the winter at Somerset Palace so they might be close to court without incurring the great costs. The palace had fallen somewhat into disrepair, but they were making it their own.

Charles had come to join them as well. Margaret was now unwilling to let him out of her sight. He had his tutors and his friends with him, so he did not mind his doting mother coddling him a bit.

News was coming from Scotland about infighting. Moray's stranglehold on the council had weakened and there were rumors of rebellion brewing. It came as no surprise then when her husband rushed into her rooms, a piece of parchment clutched in his hands tightly.

"He's been assassinated! Shot dead in the street."

"Who?" Margaret was near to fainting. She imagined it was her grandson.

"Moray, at Linlithgow. I have just been given the news from Cecil. I am going to see her majesty at once."

"And James? He is safe?"

"I imagine so or Cecil would have said something. I cannot imagine what is happening right now. He must be so frightened. He is just a child. And who is in power now?" All these questions were streaming out of his mouth as he ran about the room, searching for this and that. A pin for his hat, his new boots. Elizabeth hated to see people looking unpresentable.

"Please let me know as soon as you can," Margaret said from her sick bed. She was in bed with a headache that made her eyes water. She had been unable to sleep for two days. Now her heart pounded so fast she wondered if it would give out.

---

He returned later that night. His spirits still dampened but he looked less frightful. Greeting her with a kiss, he pulled up a chair by her bedside. Even by the candlelight, he looked pale and sickly.

"Dearest, you should be resting in bed as well," she said, her voice low.

"I am afraid that I shall never rest in this life," he

sighed. "Shall I tell you everything? I know how impatient you must be."

"Yes, please do so."

"The Earl of Mar has written to Elizabeth, asking for her help and advice in picking a suitable replacement for Moray. I had feared that she might take this chance to have Mary reinstated in power, but she does not wish to set her free. She is still dealing out punishments in the north, as you know. She has suggested I might go to Scotland and offer myself as an option. At the very least I can ensure the Hamiltons don't dig their claws into King James. The assassin was caught and was working alone, he was not part of a bigger plot to take control of the King, and that is our saving grace but we must act quickly."

Margaret nodded her expression as grave as his. "But how? There is no money. I had to sell off a string of pearls to settle some debts in Yorkshire. It might be another two or three years before we could even think of doing this."

Matthew shrugged. "I shall have to ask the Queen for more money. If she wishes for me to go, she will have to pay."

"She will know you desire to go above all else and will delay until you are forced to borrow money. I will write to Cecil," she said, a hand going up to her forehead as a fresh burst of pain flooded over her. "We are two sickly elderly people now, but we shall have to gather our strength."

He took her hand and gave it a squeeze. "Shall I send for the doctor to prescribe you another draft?"

"No point. They haven't cured me before. Send for my writing desk. I won't be able to sleep until this is done."

---

"The Queen has been excommunicated by the Pope," Margaret told Matthew. She had been visiting Elizabeth at court and was there when the news arrived. Leicester swore aloud at the news but Elizabeth had merely smiled. Though her eyes had seemed to darken.

Margaret knew she wasn't very concerned. Her subjects were loyal but she wondered if any foreign power would take this chance to invade. That's where the true risk lay. This was also their chance.

Elizabeth would wish to shore up support in Scotland and make sure that they wouldn't make alliances with France or Spain. She would look even more favorably on Matthew now.

After the May Day celebrations, which were grand and featured pageants that started in the morning and lasted well into the night, they received the news they had been waiting to hear.

"I am to go," Matthew said, holding out the official document to her. "With the Queen's blessing. I have been named Lieutenant General of Scotland, with promises that my lands will be restored to me once again. I have not been named regent yet, but I shall be able to take charge of James and ensure his safety."

"Thank God! This is what we've been hoping for, isn't it?"

"Yes, and I am sure that they shall vote for me to be regent. I have it on good authority that the Queen is pressing Morton and Mar to back me."

"Why do you seem so sullen then?"

"Because I fear I am not up to the task and it means that once again I must leave you and Charles. Who knows what trouble you will get up to in my absence?"

She chuckled at that.

"But think of how lucky you are to be with James and watch over him. You can appoint the best tutors and make sure he knows what happened to his father. He will bring his murderers to justice if we cannot."

"And if I'd rather be with you?" He pulled her close. "I want to die in your arms, in my own bed. I am too old to go off fighting wars. I should be easing into retirement. Why couldn't this have come to me sooner?"

"Now now," she scolded him. "You shall live for many years yet. I command it. And I shall petition Queen Elizabeth to let me go with you. Perhaps you will even bring King James here on a state visit."

He kissed her, both knowing that what she said was impossible.

She watched it happen as though through a fog. Everything was to be packed up and ready for travel north. William Knockes came asking for money to buy new tresses for the hawks that he was to take with him. Richard Norton came with an outline of the travel plans and the costs that would be required.

It was the priest John Kay that was to go to Scotland with him. Margaret had the feeling he should take more than just the one.

She looked at these men with such envy that she could not bring herself to meet their eyes. They were going where she could not follow, though it was her heart's desire.

Suddenly, she had a strong desire to put ink to paper once more. In her youth she had dabbled in poetry, letters to lovers. As a married woman she had no need for poems. Being around Matthew was enough. But now, yet again, she was to be alone and this time she had the dreadful feeling she would not live to see him return.

She bid him goodbye, weeping so much she had to dig her finger into a pin on her dress until it bled so she could get a coherent word out.

"Be at peace, my wife. We shall be reunited." He kissed her. His lips lingered longer than they should until their son's awkward cough behind him made him pull back.

"Go with my blessing and love. We shall be here awaiting news and your return. Dearest Mathieu, write to me often?"

"I swear, I shall." He placed a hand over his heart.

She stepped back and watched him lay his hand on his son's head in blessing. She could not hear the words he spoke to him. Her Charles seemed doomed to be raised without both his parents.

As the large retinue rode off up to the great north road, she stayed until the dust on the road settled.

Neither her lady in waiting nor her chaplain could convince her to go inside.

That night she picked up the pen and wrote the first of many letters to her husband, the love of her life and the cause of so much heartache. She began with a poem...

> *"The northern wind*
>> *Has turned his mind*
>> *And blown him clear away,*
>> *Whereby my heart,*
>> *My mirth, my health,*
>> *Has turned to great decay."*

# AFTERWORD

Margaret Douglas did not live to see if any of her ambitions came to fruition. Her husband became regent but was shortly assassinated after assuming power. They never met again, though they wrote often to each other, and he entrusted her above all others to give Queen Elizabeth and the English council news from Scotland.

Though heartbroken, Margaret would not stop scheming to advance her family and press her claims. Along with Bess of Hardwick, they plotted the secret marriage of their children. As a result, Margaret found herself once again locked away in the Tower and was finally released upon her son Charles's death. He had one daughter before dying, named Arabella Stuart, whose own short life was rife with intrigue, tragedies and secret love affairs.

Margaret died, severely in debt, shortly after her son Charles in 1578 at the age of 62. She would have been happy to know that one of her schemes would succeed. Upon Elizabeth's death, Margaret's grandson James also became King of England, as well as Scotland and Ireland.

Made in the USA
Middletown, DE
19 September 2023